*Sydney turned her face into his neck and laid her head against his shoulder. Her breath whispered across his skin.*

Danny's breath caught in his throat and his heart stuttered. It would be so easy to draw her down onto the blanket they shared, to explore the feminine treasures of her body—

What was he thinking? A rogue wave of longing surged high and swept over him, urging him to drop his head and set his mouth against her soft pink lips. He wanted it so badly. Releasing her, he surged to his feet. "Well. We should get going if you want to see the rest of the island's attractions."

"Actually, I'm getting tired. It probably would be best if I went back and took a nap."

Danny hadn't imagined he'd ever feel such a strong need to make love again. It was almost a relief to know his body still yearned for feminine contact. But he didn't need Sydney, he reminded himself forcefully. He didn't need anyone, and the last thing he wanted was to be any more involved in her life than he already was.

## ANNE MARIE WINSTON

RITA® Award finalist and bestselling author Anne Marie Winston loves babies she can give back when they cry, animals in all shapes and sizes and just about anything that blooms. When she's not writing, she's managing a house full of animals and teenagers, reading anything she can find and trying *not* to eat chocolate. She will dance at the slightest provocation and weeds her gardens when she can't see the sun for the weeds anymore.

Working with other authors on a large-scale story line is always challenging and exciting. This one was particularly special to Anne Marie because she had the opportunity to work with Karen Rose Smith, one of her first friends "in the business." Karen and Anne Marie sold their first books within one week of each other more than a decade ago. You can learn more about Anne Marie's novels by visiting her Web site at www.annemariewinston.com.

# LOGAN'S LEGACY

# THE HOMECOMING
## ANNE MARIE WINSTON

Silhouette Books

Published by Silhouette Books
**America's Publisher of Contemporary Romance**

Special thanks and acknowledgment are given to Anne Marie Winston for her contribution to the LOGAN'S LEGACY series.

 SILHOUETTE BOOKS

ISBN 0-373-61395-4

THE HOMECOMING

Visit Silhouette Books at www.eHarlequin.com

**Printed in U.S.A.**

Be a part of

# Logan's Legacy

*Because birthright has its privileges
and family ties run deep.*

On an island retreat, a lost man encounters a
woman claiming to know his kidnapped son.
Will redemption and love touch them both?

**Sydney Aston:** Her adopted son's history
was mysterious, so she went on a quest to
find his biological family. When she encountered
Danny Crosby, she fell in love with him and wrestled
with her heart. He had to know the truth—that his
beloved son was still alive!

**Danny Crosby:** A broken man after his son's
disappearance, Danny led a reclusive life. But Sydney
brought him back into the world...and back to the
son he'd ached for all these years. Would he be given
a second chance at having a family?

**A Logan Reunion:** The Logans visit their long-lost
son and vow to help the sweet boy robbed from them
so many years ago. Robbie Logan has finally come
home.

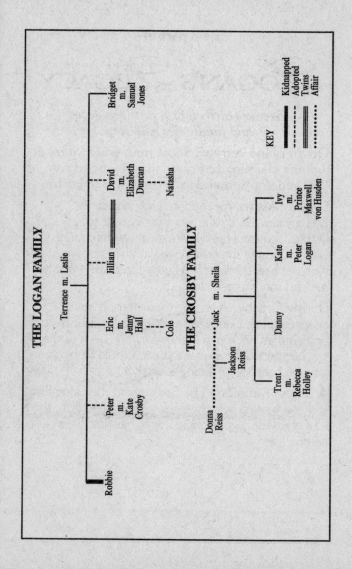

# THE LOGAN FAMILY

Terrence m. Leslie

Robbie

Peter
m.
Kate
Crosby

Eric
m.
Jenny
Hall

Cole

Jillian ═══ David
m.
Elizabeth
Duncan

Natasha

Bridget
m.
Samuel
Jones

# THE CROSBY FAMILY

Donna ·········· Jack  m.  Sheila
Reiss

Jackson
Reiss

Trent
m.
Rebecca
Holley

Danny

Kate
m.
Peter
Logan

Ivy
m.
Prince
Maxwell
von Husden

KEY

▬▬▬▬  Kidnapped
------  Adopted
═══  Twins
··········  Affair

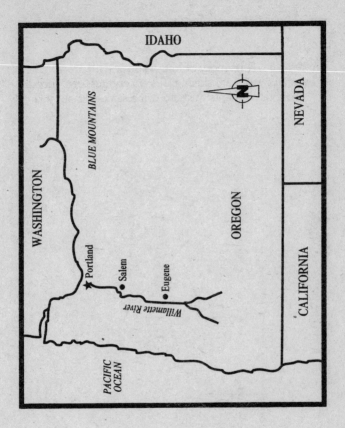

In memory of Katrina Sue Smith.
I wish we still were sharing life's adventures, dear friend.
"Precious moments" just aren't the same without you.

# One

*The dream started as it always did. Danny's best friend was walking away with the strange man.*

*Danny was afraid. Their teacher, Miss Hanley, always told them never to get in a car with strangers. She said if they were only going to learn one thing in first grade, that was the one they should learn. Even Danny's mother, who didn't seem to care what he did as long as he stayed out of her way, had made him promise never to go anywhere with anyone other than his dad or her without permission.*

*Danny ran into his house, yelling for his mother. She could stop Robbie. If he could just find his mother, she could help his friend.*

*But she wasn't in the kitchen, or the living room, or anywhere. He called and called but she never answered him.*

*He frantically rushed back outside. There! A lady. One of the neighbors walking down the street. Danny rushed up to her, heedless of the tears streaking his cheeks. "Help me, please," he cried. "A bad man's taking my friend!"*

*But the lady didn't even look down at him, and he realized suddenly that it wasn't his neighbor. It wasn't anybody he knew, and she wouldn't look at him, wouldn't talk to him.*

*Another man approached and Danny asked him for help, but the man kept on going as if he hadn't even heard him. Danny repeated his actions with each passerby, growing ever more frantic as person after person brushed him off and kept going. He could hear himself sobbing, "Help me, please help my friend."*

*Then he heard a voice behind him. "I'll help you. Come with me."*

*Danny turned around, relief almost a physical thing rushing through him. But as his gaze focused on the face of the man standing there with his hand outstretched, shock and fear erased the relief.*

*The bad man stood right behind him. Danny was too terrified to move. All he could do was watch as the man reached for him—*

Danny Crosby woke with a shout, sitting bolt upright in his bed. Or had it been a scream? His staff

would wonder what was going on in his bedroom at—
he glanced at the glowing face of the bedside clock—
six in the morning. He raised his hands and scrubbed
them over his face, dragging back his thick hair. God,
that nightmare had been worse than usual, as bad as it
had been when he was much, much younger.

His heart was racing and he felt hot and sweaty, unable to stay in bed a moment longer. He only had
nightmares about once a month these days, but he
knew from long experience there was no point in at-
tempting to go back to sleep.

Throwing back the light cover, he rose and walked
naked through the wide French doors onto the terrace
outside his bedroom. He owned the whole island of
Nanilani, less than a mile off the southern coast of
Kauai island; there was no one around to see him. It
was a typically clear and lovely early-July night in the
Hawaiian Islands, the temperature hovering in the sev-
enties, although he barely noticed. The beauty of the
setting amid which he'd chosen to spend the rest of his
life was overlaid by the harsh memories he'd never
been able to escape.

He automatically patted his chest for a cigarette,
then remembered that he wasn't wearing anything.
And even more importantly, he'd quit smoking when
he'd entered rehab well over a decade ago. Even after
Noah and Felicia— He cut off the thought before it
could go any further. There was a limit to how many
kinds of mental torture he could endure in one night.

He raised a hand to pat his pocket again but caught

the gesture in midair. Some habits died harder than others. He supposed it was a good thing that cigarettes were all he felt the need for after that damned dream.

He took a deep breath and focused his jangled nerves, letting himself be hypnotized by the rolling surf he could see from the lanai.

Below the outcropping of black volcanic rock that fell away from the edge of the terrace, the sea rolled in against the edges of his beach in rhythmic curls of white that disintegrated as they smashed against the shallow slope that marked the water's edge. The sand was lighter than the rocks. Black sand beaches were more common in the eastern part of the islands, which were still young and growing, thanks to their active volcanoes. True black sand was created as an explosive result of molten lava entering cool sea water. The reaction literally pulverized the lava. Here on Nanilani, as on the other islands at the northwestern end of the chain, the islands' growth had stopped eons ago.

It wasn't really *his* beach in a personal sense. Brian Summers, the real estate developer back in Portland, had been quite clear about that when he'd found the special piece of secluded property that he'd thought would meet Danny's needs. All beaches in Hawaii technically were public property, but he owned the rest of the island so there was no access except by sea. And since the beaches of Nanilani were neither exceptionally safe nor exceptionally beautiful compared to some of the state's most famous, he rarely had to worry about tour boats stopping for any length of time.

Of course, beauty was a relative term in Hawaii, where every place you looked were lovely and breathtaking views. Even the name of his island referred to it: *nani* was the Hawaiian word for beautiful, and *lani* referred to the sky or heaven. Nanilani: beautiful heaven. Danny sincerely doubted it was possible to buy an ugly piece of property here.

He'd been unbelievably lucky three years ago; when he'd asked Brian to find him an isolated home in the islands, the Robinson family who owned Ni'ihau and part of Kauai were selling Nanilani.

Suddenly he realized what he'd just been thinking. He'd been lucky? Having his son abducted and his wife kill herself wasn't the kind of luck he'd wish on anyone. Abandoning thought, he purposely emptied his mind and focused again on the view before him. The breakers rolling in from the ocean were hypnotizing in their endless rhythm. The surf was incredibly powerful here where there were no reefs to slow their approach to land. How many times had he stood down there on that beach and contemplated simply walking into the water until those waves sucked him under?

Plenty. But he'd gone the route of self-destruction in his past and he'd never do it again. Trent would be devastated. And Danny would cut off his arm rather than hurt his older brother, who'd dragged him back from the brink four times already if Danny counted getting him out of that hellish military school, bugging their father Jack to find him when he'd subsequently done his disappearing act, getting him into counseling after that one halfhearted overdose and finally, dragging him back into the company business after Noah and Felicia were gone. The last might not sound like the action of a savior but it had been: it had given Danny a purpose and a focus that had kept him sane throughout the darkest days of his life. He'd sworn he would never let Trent down again, and he wouldn't. Not in the business and not in any other way.

*Damn it, Dan, you're thinking again.* He wasn't having much success with his mind-emptying meditation today.

To the left, the beach disappeared in a seemingly endless ribbon of sand that he knew from experience went on for miles before it came up against a rock cliff. These older islands also had more beach than the younger ones. On his right, not nearly as far away, another such cliff cut off his beach abruptly. Its base was strewn with dark boulders that had crumbled from the main body of the rock eons ago when earthquakes beneath the sea floor had heaved the rock upward. Like Kauai and Ni'ihau, Nanilani was among the oldest of the existing islands in the Hawaiian chain, with no volcanic activity. All that remained of the earth's ancient contortions were the black rock and red dirt upon which much of the island was built.

Below him, a scattering of the broken boulders rose from the sea while others lay on the sand, deceptively small from up here. He'd stood on those boulders and he knew many of them were significantly taller than he was.

The waves frothed and churned around the base of the cliff and surged in to smack at the boulders, boiling up around them to the beach. Something caught his eye and he frowned, trying to focus more clearly. Atop one of the smaller boulders lay something light-colored and out of place. He knew this view, had looked out on it for over three years now. Whatever that was, it wasn't part of the natural scenery.

He studied the shape of the lighter blob, mildly puzzled. There hadn't been a storm to toss anything up that high out of the water's reach.

Then his brain clicked into focus and he realized the shape was a person!

The revelation hadn't even completely jelled in his consciousness as he bolted back inside and snagged a pair of ragged denim shorts from the chair where he'd tossed them when he went to bed. He stepped into the cutoffs and zipped them. Then he ripped the cover from his bed before he raced from his room. Pausing briefly outside the door to shove his feet into his reef shoes, he ran to the stone steps that led from his terrace to the path down the cliff.

Where the hell had the person come from? The figure hadn't been moving. Please, God, don't let him be dead. More people drowned each year in this state than anywhere else in the country. And even if he hadn't drowned, he could be hypothermic if he'd been in the water long enough. Hawaiian waters might be temperate but a prolonged dip in the Pacific when the sun wasn't out wouldn't have been a pleasant experience. If indeed, the person had been in the water. He had assumed that was the case, since he hadn't seen a boat.

As he descended, he could see the lights of Kauai, the northernmost of the main Hawaiian chain and his nearest neighbor, twinkling in the distance. Had the person been sailing from there and gotten lost?

Reaching the bottom of the steps, he raced across the soft, dry sand, which still held the warmth of the day before. The boulders to the right were much farther away than they looked from the bird's-eye view he had from the house, and he pushed through the soft sand until he hit the hard-packed surface near the water's edge. Then he settled into a fast but steady pace, much as he did during his daily morning runs.

As he ran, his mind continued to work. It occurred to him that he'd been stupid to run out of the house without one of the portable intercom devices he'd bought. Only two people lived with him on the island, an older native Hawaiian couple who had worked for the previous owner and had proved highly satisfactory to Danny. They had a large family of children and grandchildren who came over in a motor launch several times a week with mail and food and other supplies. Occasionally a couple of them would stay for a few days, but for the most part, it was just Danny and Leilani and Johnny.

Leilani cooked and kept the house clean while her husband did a fine job keeping the house and grounds in top shape. People outside the family called him Big

John and the name was well deserved. He had the deceptively beefy build of the native Hawaiian people; he was actually far more muscle than fat. If the person on the rocks was badly hurt, Danny would go back and enlist Johnny to help him get the guy to the house.

Increasing his pace, Danny pushed himself until the boulders drew near. Now the shape on the rocks definitely looked like a person. A person who wasn't moving and didn't appear to have changed position since Danny had first seen him. *Please don't let him be dead.*

Breathing heavily, Danny scrambled up over the rocks, dropping the blanket he'd tucked beneath his arm as he reached the top. The guy was small. God, he hoped it wasn't a kid. He had a bad feeling that he might be looking at a drowning victim as he dropped to his knees at the side of the body.

Close up, he was stunned to find that the guy was really a woman. She lay on her stomach with her head turned to one side, her brown hair flung out around her head. It wasn't dripping but certainly was still wet. The hair partly covered her face and all he could see was the curve of her cheek and a small straight nose.

Rivulets of water had run out of her shorts and shirt and down the sides of the rock. Though it appeared she'd been there long enough for the excess water to drain away, she still was soaking wet, confirming what he'd thought earlier. She must have been on a boat from one of the other islands. Kauai, almost certainly, since Ni'ihau was populated only by a small village of native people. Although why a tourist would come out on the ocean alone escaped him.

He was sure she wasn't local. What gave her away was the color of her skin. His unmoving guest was paler than the golden sand he'd just run across. And she didn't look badly sunburned, so she must not have gotten onto these rocks until sometime after dark last night.

A tourist out alone at night?

Placing a tentative hand on one out-flung arm, he nearly sagged with relief. The arm wasn't cold as in corpse-cold, and beneath the delicate wrist he could feel a pulse. Not strong, but far from thready and faint, either.

He bent over until his ear was near her mouth. Thank God she was breathing as well. Slowly and steadily, with no sign that she might stop.

Gingerly he started running his hands over her arms and legs, noting that she seemed slender and well-muscled. He wasn't experienced with first aid and probably wouldn't know a broken bone unless it was an obvious fracture, but nothing seemed out of the ordinary to him.

She had very pretty skin, he noted with absent appreciation. Smooth and silky, but a little too cool. He shook out the blanket and carefully tucked it around her. If she was in shock, he knew it was important to keep her warm.

"Hey," he said, reluctant to move her. He placed a hand on her upper arm, a little surprised to see how big his own hand looked in contrast. "Miss? Wake up. Talk to me, please?"

He didn't want to move her, knew he shouldn't turn her over. Since she seemed all right, he should go and call for help, then come back. But he hated to leave while she was unconscious. What if she woke up and there was nobody here? She could wander off in the wrong direction.

If she didn't look at just the right angle she might not see the house high above the cliff. Even if she saw the house, she would have no notion how to get to it. And if she wasn't fully cognizant of her situation, she might not even realize that the blanket meant some-one had found her and would return.

Just then she groaned, and the sound instantly solved his dilemma. He couldn't leave her if she was about to wake up.

She groaned again, stirring, and he placed a cautionary hand on her back when she made feeble motions as if to get up.

"Don't try to move yet," he said. Beneath his hand, he felt her slender frame relax. Moving his hand sooth-ingly over her back in little circles much as he'd done with his infant son when he'd had him, he added, "I don't know where you swam from, but there's no sign of your boat, and you might have injuries if you slammed against the rocks on your way in."

"I don't think I do," she said in a slow, puzzled voice that was pleasantly husky. "Nothing feels bro-ken." She was silent for a moment. Finally, she said, "I was in a boat?"

"I was hoping you could tell me." For the first time

it occurred to him that she might not have been alone. "Can you remember if there was anyone else with you?" God, he'd better check around and make sure there wasn't someone else lying injured and helpless down here.

She was silent. Finally, she said in a small voice, "I don't remember."

Giving the area a visual scan, Danny saw no other body on the rocks or shore. Why, then, had this tourist gone out on the ocean alone? Even a native would be unlikely to take a risk like that.

As if she'd read his thoughts, she said, "I took boats out on the r-river all my life." Her teeth chattered despite the warmth of the dawning day. "But the ocean's a lot different."

"Yeah," he said dryly. "The ocean's a lot different from a river." He tried not to think of what could have happened to her had she not fetched up on his rocks. More than one person had gotten caught in the strong currents that ran from the Hawaiian Islands straight across the Pacific with not a speck of land for hundreds of miles. Others, without boats, had been discovered by the sharks that frequented the waters.

He was about to ask her what river she'd meant when she made another bid to get up, and this time he decided he might as well let her try. He moved back, and she rolled to her side, then came up into a sitting position with her knees drawn up. "Oh," she said. "Dizzy."

From this angle, he could see why. There was a

large and ugly knot just above her right temple with blood still oozing from the broken skin at its center. Looking down, he saw that the rock against which her head had lain was dark with blood.

His stomach lurched. "You've got a pretty hefty bump on your head," he said, trying to stay calm, though his mind was racing, wondering how much blood she'd lost. *Calm down,* he told himself, *everybody knows head wounds bleed like crazy and look worse than they usually are.* "Looks like one of those rocks reached out and smacked you on the way in."

She probably would be pretty, he thought, cleaned up with a little color in her face. She had nice cheekbones to go with that cute little nose, and although her lips were nearly blue, they were nicely shaped and full. She had closed her eyes on sitting up and he hadn't gotten even a glimpse of their color, but the lashes that shielded them lay across her cheeks like tiny fronds of a thickly feathered fern.

One corner of her mouth had turned up at his words, but he could see that she was swallowing and breathing deeply, probably fighting nausea.

"I'm Danny," he said, talking just so she wouldn't feel compelled to respond. "This island is my home. I imagine you came over from Kauai sometime late yesterday and got caught in the currents."

"Yes. Caught in the currents." Her voice was faint but definite from beneath the fall of thick hair that fell forward around her bent head as she raised her arms and wrapped them around her raised knees. "Pushed me toward a reef."

"From Kauai?"

She hesitated. Her shoulders rose and fell. "I'm not sure," she admitted.

He blinked. It was common, he'd heard, for people with head injuries to forget things temporarily. Especially things that happened right before their accidents.

"What's your name?" he asked her, still kneeling beside her.

She raised her head cautiously, clearly testing her stomach as she opened her mouth to reply, but then an odd expression crossed her face. She automatically whipped her head around to face him, but immediately winced and dropped it back to her knees. "I— My name is— I don't know!" She sounded both astonished and bewildered. "Just give me a minute. I'm just a little…a little…I don't know who I am!"

Her eyes were blue. Very blue at the moment, the irises encircled by dark rings that only made them more compelling. "Okay. Relax. I'm sure it'll come to you in a moment," he said soothingly. "We'll just stay here for a little while and when you feel better I'll take you to my house." He hoped Johnny would show up long before that since Danny was pretty sure his nameless guest wasn't up to taking a stroll along the beach. "Can you look straight at me?" he asked as he moved around in front of her.

"Why?" But she did as he asked.

"I want to check your pupils."

"Oh."

They looked fine to him, and he thanked God for that. If they'd been unequal in size, he'd have known something serious was wrong.

He glanced at his watch surreptitiously. Twenty minutes to wait. Leilani would be expecting him for breakfast around seven. When he didn't show up and wasn't in the house by then, she would send Johnny to look for him. And since he always ran along the beach before breakfast, the first thing Johnny would do would be to come down the cliff, and Danny would be able to send him back up the hill for something resembling a stretcher. Even though he was in the best shape of his life and the woman beside him looked slender and small-boned, he knew he couldn't carry her along the beach and up the cliff path alone.

His thoughts were distracted as she put her palms on the ground and prepared to shift her weight onto her feet.

"You probably shouldn't move," he said. "I have someone who can help me carry you up to the house in a few minutes."

"I'm too big to carry," she said, her lips curving up as if that was extraordinarily funny. "I can walk." She pushed herself up farther and before he could prevent it, she'd stood up.

Danny stood up, too, fast. He grabbed for her when she started to slide sideways. She was oddly boneless and for a moment he thought she'd passed out as she flopped against him, her head falling into the curve of his shoulder. "Whoa," he said.

"Sorry." She sounded as if she'd clenched her teeth together.

"Why don't you sit back down?" he suggested. "It's a long walk down the beach to the stairs, and a long, steep climb up to the house. My groundskeeper will be coming this way in a little while and he'll be able to help."

She was taller than he'd expected, fitting neatly against his own six-foot frame. Felicia had been short. When they'd danced together, not that they'd ever danced much, he'd got a crick in his neck from looking down at her.

Pain lanced through him. He hadn't imagined he'd ever hold a woman in his arms again. He hadn't wanted to. All he wanted was to be left alone.

"...probably should sit down again. Everything's sort of whirling around me as if I were on a merry-go-round. Sorry. I have this habit of thinking I have to do everything myself."

"It's all right." He struggled to keep his tone level. This poor woman couldn't even remember her own name. She didn't need to be saddled with his problems. He lowered her to the boulder, alarmed again at the way her arms flopped down when he pulled them from around his neck.

She sat very still for a moment. "Wow," she said. "My head is killing me. I must have met a rock head-first."

"As soon as we get up to the house," he said, "I'll call a doctor."

"You could just drop me at the nearest hospital," she said. "I don't want to be a burden, and I think I probably should get my head looked at."

He cleared his throat. "This is a private island," he said. "There is no hospital."

"No...? You're kidding." She knew better than to move her head this time. "Then how are you going to call a doctor?"

His lips quirked but she had her eyes closed again so she didn't see his amusement. "I'll manage."

She couldn't know that he was so filthy rich he could probably call an entire medical staff over if he wanted. But then the amusement fled. If he had to choose between the Crosby fortune that his father had amassed and having his wife and son back again, he'd give away every dime. He shot to his feet. "Stay here," he said. "I'll go and hurry my friend along and we'll be back to take you up to the house."

She was in pain, but he was pretty sure she wasn't seriously disoriented. She'd sounded pretty rational and he thought she understood.

Then again, he thought as he climbed back down off the boulder and began to lope along the tide line, she didn't even know her own name right now.

# Two

Johnny was coming down the steps as Danny ran back toward the house. The two men retraced Danny's steps to where the young woman waited, then carried her up to the house in a sling made of the blanket.

Danny put her in a first-floor sitting room, then called over to Kauai. First he spoke to a doctor, who agreed to come over and examine the woman. The man was a relative of Johnny's—no surprise there—and Danny had met him before.

Then he called the Kauai Police Department in Lihu'e and asked for the chief. Another relative of Johnny's, the chief had welcomed him when he'd first come to the island, though Danny had had no reason to call the department before.

After a cordial greeting, Danny said, "Are you missing any female tourists?"

There was a slight pause and Danny could almost feel the man putting on his official hat. "Why do you ask?"

"I found a woman this morning—"

"Alive?"

"Yes. She's in good shape, just a little banged up. I have a doctor coming over to look at her. Your cousin Eddie, as a matter of fact."

The chief chuckled. "Dat Eddie, he take care your little wahine."

Danny was familiar with the interesting brand of pidgin spoken in the islands. He knew the chief would never dream of using it with a tourist or a stranger and he felt oddly flattered. "I hope so," he said. "She's having a little trouble remembering how she got here." *And by the way, she doesn't know her name, either.*

As if he were reading Danny's mind, the chief said, "Sydney Aston. She was staying at the Marriott on Kalapaki Beach. Yesterday she went over to Waimea and rented a boat out of Kikialoa Harbor."

"Alone?" He couldn't believe anyone would let a young, single female tourist take a boat out alone.

"Alone." The chief's voice held a grim note now. "Ronny Kamehana said he'd take her out. She wanted to go cruisin' past your island. But Ronny drink too much and when she pay up front and say she know boats, he let her go."

"I might make a point of coming over there and kicking Ronny Kamehana's butt one of these days," Danny said in an equally grim tone. "That woman could have died."

"Don' worry. Ronny goin' be sorry," the chief said. "Besides, his boat gone now, yeah?"

"Yeah. Make sure he doesn't get another one."

"So what you goin' to do with your guest? You want Eddie bring her back?"

"No," said Danny, "unless she needs urgent medical attention, she can stay here for a day or two until she feels a little better. She's going to be pretty sore for a while, I imagine." He didn't really know why he didn't just ship her off with Eddie. But he was the one who had found her, and ever since she'd looked at him with those wide blue eyes, he'd wanted to talk to her more.

"Okay," said the chief. "I'll let the hotel know where she is. The manager was pretty worried when she was gone all night."

*"Mahalo,"* said Danny formally. Thank you.

"You're welcome," said the chief in return. "And thank you for your help. Keep me posted."

Danny hung up the phone and headed for his room to shower and shave. Leilani had taken charge of the guest when he and Johnny had brought her in, and he knew she was in good hands.

Sydney, he thought. Sydney was in good hands.

* * *

An hour later Johnny's cousin Eddie came up the path from the dock on one of the ATVs kept for that purpose. Dr. Eddie Atada was a native Hawaiian success story. He'd gotten a scholarship to Stanford and then gone to medical school before coming back to Hawaii and establishing a practice on his home island of Kauai.

"Howzit?" he inquired when Danny met him at the door, shaking Danny's hand with such vigor that Danny wondered if he'd need a cast when Eddie was done. Eddie was nearly as tall as Johnny and only slightly less stocky in build. He could easily have been a lineman for any pro football team due to his size alone.

"It's going well," Danny said, "except for finding strange women washed up on the beach."

Eddie laughed, a booming sound that echoed through the wide hallway. "Not such a bad thing, yeah?"

Danny grinned, but made no answer. "She's back here," he said, leading the way to the room to which Sydney Aston had been taken.

When he knocked on the door, Leilani's voice said, "Come in."

"The doctor's here," Danny said, stepping aside so Eddie could enter the room.

Leilani apparently had helped their guest shower, because she looked clean and fresh and her shoulder-length brown hair was shiny and nearly dry. She wore a flowered housecoat-type garment that must have belonged to one of Leilani's grandchildren, because it was only slightly too large through the shoulders.

"Hello," she said.

"I'll wait out here while you examine her," Danny said to Eddie, suiting action to his words.

He waited in the hallway, hearing the rise and fall of lighter female tones interspersed with Eddie's rumbling chuckles. Finally, the door opened and Eddie came back into the hallway.

"How is she?" Danny asked.

"Let's sit down." Eddie walked back along the hallway until he came to the living room, where he proceeded to park his bulk in one of the comfortable overstuffed chairs.

"Are you going to give me bad news?" Danny tried for flippancy but it didn't quite come off. Bad news was his middle name.

Eddie regarded him soberly, no teasing glint in his eye now. "You didn't tell me she can't remember her name," he said.

"I thought maybe it would come to her once she was calm and settled." Danny regarded the doctor anxiously. "You don't think it's permanent, do you?"

"I doubt it. Long-term amnesia is very rare. But often after head injuries patients lose chunks of time surrounding the accident that they never recall. She may never be able to tell you how she got on your beach."

"She's already remembered bits and pieces of that."

"That's a good sign," Eddie said. "All she really needs is peace and quiet. She'd be better off here than at a hotel. And I really wouldn't recommend she fly home right away. The whole traveling thing is stressful enough when you're well, much less when you've just landed headfirst on a piece of prime Hawaiian real estate."

Danny smiled because the other man seemed to require it.

"Don't worry," Eddie said. "I'll bet that after a few restful days here her memory will return and your mystery guest will be able to tell you everything."

Everett Baker entered the law offices of Gantler & Abernathie hesitantly. The waiting area was expensively appointed, with leather chairs, some kind of pretty tables with inlaid marquetry on the tops, and rugs thicker than his mattress. He could never afford a lawyer like this. But Terrence Logan could, and he'd insisted on getting Everett the best criminal defense lawyer in Portland. The sharp edge of guilt's knife twisted in his stomach as he thought of his biological father's generosity.

There were two other people in the reception area and as he gave his name to the woman at the large desk he wondered if either one of them was an arrested criminal out on bail.

Bail. When he'd stood in that Portland courtroom and heard the hefty sum that guaranteed he wouldn't take off for Timbuktu at the first chance, he'd felt another load of despair land squarely on his shoulders. He'd never be able to raise that kind of money.

But then Terrence Logan—his father—had whispered in the bailiff's ear, the bailiff had approached the judge, and the next thing Everett knew he was walking out into the warm Oregon air, a temporarily free man. He'd looked at the man who had signed his bail bond and said, "Why?" although it barely squeaked out past the lump in his throat.

Terrence Logan had smiled, and the warmth in his eyes made Everett feel even worse than he already did. "Because you're my son," he'd said.

*But I tried to ruin your adoption foundation!* Everett wanted to say. *I'm not worthy to be called your son.* But the words wouldn't come. He couldn't fathom how the Logans could bear to look at him after the damage he'd helped to cause to Children's Connection. He'd been so stupid! So…gullible, lapping up Charlie's pretended friendship like a starving dog. He was pathetic. There was no way he could ever be associated with the Logans now, even if he did have that biological connection. Too much time had passed.

"Mr. Baker? Mr. Abernathie will see you now." The receptionist smiled as she stood and led him into the lawyer's office.

"Everett." Bernard Abernathie crossed the room to shake his hand and guide him toward a chair before his desk. "I bet it feels good to be a free man again."

Everett nodded. "But I shouldn't be."

"And you probably wouldn't be," the man said

sharply, "if you'd continued on with that harebrained notion of representing yourself. I'm glad you've decided to accept your parents' offer."

Everett shrugged. "I didn't want to hurt their feelings."

The lawyer nodded, clasping his hands together. "Whatever your reasons, it seems your parents are most interested in doing whatever they can to help you refute these charges. They've offered to pay for your legal defense."

"I can't refute the charges," Everett said dully. "I did everything they say I did."

"Yes, but it's *why* you did it that's important," Abernathie told him. "Charlie Prescott manipulated you right from the very beginning." He leaned forward and placed his hands flat on his desk, pinning Everett with his gaze. "This morning I talked with the prosecutor. Since Prescott's dead, they've come to the end of what they can accomplish in terms of recovering any of the children he stole. That Russian idiot is useless. If you'll agree to give the cops all the information you have, and if it leads to the recovery of at least some of them, you'll receive a suspended sentence during which you'll be required to attend court-appointed psychiatric counseling."

A suspended sentence. The words echoed in his head. Everett hesitated. It wasn't right, was it, that he got off unpunished? "But—"

"But nothing," his counsel said. "There's no room for nobility when you're facing prison."

Everett swallowed. "I broke the law, too."

Bernard Abernathie sighed. "Look, Everett, or Robert, or whatever you'd like to be called now. I deal with a lot of criminals. I see con artists and liars and worms every day. I represent some of them. You—" He looked Everett squarely in the eye. "—are not a hardened criminal. Jail is the wrong answer for you. If you feel you have to atone, do some kind of volunteer work. But you don't walk away from a gift like this. This is your *freedom* we're talking about here."

Everett still hesitated, evaluating Abernathie's words.

"Isn't there anything you care about enough to avoid prison?" His lawyer's voice was laced with exasperation and what sounded like a trace of compassion.

*Anything you care about.* Nancy Allen's face flashed across his mind. His heart squeezed in pain. He could never approach her again. She knew about what he'd done, knew the full story. He'd used her to gain information about the babies at Portland General Hospital. Surely she wished she'd never met him. She must hate him.

Even so, he realized he wouldn't get her out of his heart so easily. Nancy was everything good and right, the best thing that had ever happened to him in his entire life, and he'd never forget her.

Danny's unexpected visitor slept and rested most of the rest of the day. The next morning, when he went down for his first cup of coffee, Leilani said, "The young lady's awake. I could set up breakfast for the two of you on the lanai."

Danny glanced at his housekeeper sharply, hoping she wasn't having visions of matchmaking. But Leilani's broad, pretty face was serene and she met his gaze as she waited for his answer.

"I guess that would be all right," he said slowly. He wanted to talk to Sydney Aston anyway. Did she even know she was Sydney Aston yet? Eddie had warned him to let her set the pace of her recovery. If she asked, he would tell her what her name was. But he hoped she'd remember on her own.

He went out to the terrace after his workout and shower to find Leilani just seating his guest.

"Good morning," he said.

"Good morning." She smiled at him. "You know, I'm not sure I even got your name yesterday. Did you tell me you're Danny?"

He nodded, smiling in return as he extended a hand. "Daniel Dane Crosby, but everyone calls me Danny."

"Well, Daniel Dane Crosby called Danny," she said, "I owe you an enormous debt. If you hadn't seen me, I can't imagine what might have happened."

"At the very least, a really nasty sunburn," Danny said, trying to lighten the moment.

She laughed, but a moment later, her lovely face lost its glow. "I still can't remember my name."

"Eddie—Dr. Atada—says you'll probably begin to remember soon. You just need a little rest and relaxation." He poured a glass of the fresh strawberry papaya juice and offered it to her. "You're welcome to stay here as long as you like."

She smiled again, and he noticed that she had a small dimple in her left cheek. "Careful. It's so lovely here I might be tempted to stay indefinitely."

"Danny?" Leilani came to the French doors that led into the house. "You have a telephone call. From Portland," she added. "I think it's your brother."

Danny was puzzled as he excused himself to take the call. Why would Trent be calling him this early? Although, he supposed, it was late morning on the mainland's West Coast. Normally he and his brother corresponded through e-mail and instant messaging. The last time they'd spoken in person was a month ago.

He headed for the phone in his office. Picking up the handset, he punched the talk button. "Danny here."

"Danny." It was Trent, as he'd anticipated. "How are you?"

"Good," he said cautiously. "How are you?"

Trent laughed. "I'm fine. You sound like you think I'm coming through the phone to bite you."

"Well, you don't usually call unless there's something urgent," Danny pointed out. "What's up?"

Trent hesitated.

Danny felt the hairs on the back of his neck stand up. A shiver rippled down his spine. He had no idea what his brother was about to say but something in the constrained quality of that momentary silence raised every alarm he possessed. "What is it?" he demanded.

"Sit down," Trent suggested. "I have some news that is going to weaken your knees."

Danny sat. "All right. Tell me." His mouth was so dry he had to try twice before the words came out. *They found Noah's body.* He knew before Trent spoke again what his brother was going to say. His son was dead, just as he'd feared for the past four endless years.

"Robbie Logan is alive." Trent's voice was hushed.

The words didn't register for a long moment. Uncomprehending, Danny said, "It's not about Noah?"

"God, no!" Trent was suddenly more animated. "I'm sorry, Danny, I should have realized what you were thinking." More gently, he said, "There's still no news of Noah. This is about Robbie. Your friend Robbie's been found."

Robbie. Found. "But Robbie's dead." He still couldn't grasp it. "He can't be alive. He was buried a long time ago."

"Robbie Logan is alive," Trent repeated. "He's already had testing done that proves it. And, Danny, there's more. He was arrested in Portland under the name Everett Baker."

"Arrested?" He felt as if he'd followed Alice down the rabbit hole.

"Yes. Apparently he's been involved with a scheme to kidnap babies for resale to wealthy families. He worked for Children's Connection and used his contacts there to set up the snatches."

"My God." Danny was horrified. Kidnapping babies. How could he? He *was* a kidnapped child. And even worse, the Logans were ardent supporters of Children's Connection. Had he known who he was all along? Had Robbie deliberately set out to sabotage his parents' project? If he hadn't, it sure was a huge coincidence.

The talk of kidnapping and baby-snatching inevitably led to an image of his son, Noah, bald as a billiard ball, waving his little arms and squealing with pleasure as Danny lifted him high in the air. Drool glistened on his chin and several tiny white teeth were plainly visible through his grin.

True, this story was different from his own situation in that the babies were being provided to the wealthy instead of taken *from* them, but still… Where had Robbie gotten those babies in the first place? Somewhere, some parents' lives had been changed forever when their child was stolen. The similarities made his stomach churn.

"Where has he been all these years and why didn't he ever come home?" Anger was beginning to curl around the edges of the shock. "How could he let them—all of us—think he was dead?"

"From what little I know, I don't think he knew he wasn't Everett Baker until the woman he thought was his mother passed away a few years ago. He must have been treated pretty badly by the people who had him, and by the time he learned who he really was, he believed the Logans didn't care about him."

"But he was six years old when he was taken!" Danny protested. "How could he not remember his family?"

"We don't know what he went through, Danny." Trent was quietly reproving. "And you know firsthand the living hell an adult can put a kid through. Maybe he had to forget to survive."

Danny fell silent. Trent had hit a nerve. Their own mother was a sick, abusive witch. She'd damn near succeeded in making him believe he was worthless, so Trent was right: He shouldn't be judging Robbie.

*Robbie!* He couldn't believe the little boy had lived. For years they'd thought he was dead. The police had even found a child's body along the Willamette River that had been widely accepted to be Robbie's. And now here he was, alive!

He had another moment's pity for some other family still waiting in vain for their little boy to come home. Maybe now that they knew Robbie was alive, the Logans would exhume the child they'd buried. Surely DNA testing was sophisticated enough to figure out who that little victim had been.

"God," he said slowly. "This creates a host of issues to resolve, doesn't it?"

"Sure does," Trent said. "But I'm mostly concerned about how it's going to affect you."

Danny shrugged, then realized his brother couldn't see him. "I don't think it's going to, in any significant way. I mean, I'm glad he's alive, but it's not going to change my life."

"No, but it should give you hope. Doesn't it make you think it's possible that Noah is still out there somewhere?"

"I don't think about Noah," Danny said flatly. "I can't. It's terrific that the Logans have found their son, but let's face it. Most children abducted by strangers are killed within the first few hours if they aren't found." *And besides, with Noah's heart defect, he didn't have much of a chance in the first place. Even if whoever took him hadn't killed him, they wouldn't have known that he desperately needed surgery within the next year.*

What he didn't tell his brother was that he knew Noah wasn't still alive for another reason—because he'd had the misfortune to be Danny Crosby's son. Danny knew that the therapists he'd once seen would say it was ridiculous, but even now he couldn't shake the gut-deep certainty that his son's disappearance was a cosmic payback for his failure to save his little friend all those years ago. And even learning that Robbie had been found alive didn't alleviate the feeling. Because he hadn't acted quickly enough, Robbie had been through God only knew what, and he and his family had lost an entire childhood together.

He realized suddenly that there was a strained silence from the other end of the line.

"I do appreciate the call, Trent," he said. "That's really good news." And then he disconnected.

Sydney was still sitting on the lanai having a cup of decaf coffee when her rescuer returned from his telephone call. As Daniel Crosby walked toward her, she studied him from beneath her lashes.

Her host was definitely a hottie. He looked like a young god from a Greek story, with his golden hair and blue, blue eyes. And his build did nothing to detract from the image. He was tall, with wide shoulders that tapered to a slender waist and strong thighs that showed beneath the khaki shorts he wore today with a white sport shirt that hugged his chest, hinting at even more hard, muscled flesh.

She wasn't looking for a man, but if she were, she'd look twice at him.

Then she stopped with her coffee cup halfway to her lips. She'd just remembered something! She was single, she was sure of it. Not even a fiancé or a boyfriend. She didn't know how she knew it, but she did.

Then she saw Danny's face and she immediately set her new knowledge aside. "What's wrong?"

Danny resumed his seat opposite her at the lovely glass-topped table beneath the umbrella. He sighed. "My brother called with some good news. At least, it's sort of good news."

Sydney raised an eyebrow. "Well, that explains why you look as if your last friend in the world just died."

Danny looked at her strangely. "Actually, it's the very opposite of that."

She was intrigued by the statement, and by the air of melancholy that surrounded the handsome man. She'd noticed even through yesterday's somewhat muddled impressions that Danny rarely smiled. The corners of his mouth turned up a little when something amused him, but his expressions were nearly all variations on a sober theme. What could make a man look like that?

"I'm sorry," Danny was saying. "You have enough to worry about. How's your head feeling?"

But she wasn't going to abandon his moment of sharing, regardless of whether he regretted it. Danny needed someone to talk to, she was certain. It would be a small thing to do in return for what he'd done for her. "My head's fine," she said firmly. "Tell me what you meant about your friend."

Danny hesitated. One long finger traced the rim of his saucer over and over in a gesture she doubted he even knew he was making. "When I was six years old," he said at last, "my best friend was abducted. A man took him right out of my front yard."

She was horrified both by the revelation and by what he hadn't said. "Did you see it happen?" she asked carefully.

He nodded.

"Oh, dear heaven." Without thinking she reached out and placed her hand atop his. "I'm so sorry."

He looked surprised as his gaze locked on her face. "Thank you," he said. "It was a tough thing to go through."

"I can't imagine," she responded. When he didn't speak, she prompted, "You said you had some good news."

He nodded. "Apparently, my friend has been found alive. He was living under another name."

"Wow." Realizing she was still holding his hand, she released him and tried unobtrusively to draw her own hand back across the table. "That *is* good news."

"Yes, but he's been accused of being involved in a kidnapping ring."

She shook her head, speechless. Every time he revealed something new, she was sure her mouth was hanging open. "Well," she finally said, "I can see why you aren't sure it's good news. Does his family know?"

"Trent didn't say. But I'm sure they must. That's part of what's so awful. They held a funeral for him—or at least for a child they thought was him—years ago. And the kidnapping ring has been targeting an adoption and fertility clinic called Children's Connection, which his parents, the Logans, have supported in a big way."

*Children's Connection.* The name hit her like a bolt from a clear blue sky. She must have made some sound or expression of shock, because Danny leaned forward, looking alarmed. "What's wrong?"

"Children's Connection is in Portland. Attached to the hospital."

This time he was the one who took her hand in a strong grip. "That's right! You remember that? What else?"

"I—I'm not from Portland, I'm from Washington state. But I moved to Portland several years ago." She felt as if she were swimming underwater with her eyes open, seeing things with the blurred vision the water produced. "And I'm Sydney, Sydney…Aston!" she said triumphantly.

Danny was squeezing her hand tightly and she turned her fingers up without thinking and laced them through his. "That's terrific," he said. "You're remembering."

He didn't sound entirely surprised, and she paused in the middle of the returning memories to glance at him. "You knew already, didn't you?"

"Only your name," he said. "I didn't know you lived in Portland. That's interesting. My family is from Portland."

"Crosby," she said, her eyes widening. "You're one of the Crosby Systems Crosbys?"

"Yeah." His lips curved upward in that intriguing little smile. "I guess I am."

"How weird is that, that I should be rescued by someone from my own city?" She shook her head. "How did you know my name, anyway?"

"When I called the police to report finding you, your hotel had reported a woman of your description missing. But the doctor didn't think I should prompt you."

"The Marriott," she said promptly. "So they know I'm all right?" Then something else floated to the surface of her mind. "Good heavens, I've got to call my mother. She'll be frantic, not hearing from me in two days. She's keeping my son. I have a son! Nicholas." She smiled crookedly, feeling tears rise. "I can't believe I forgot him. He's five and he's wonderful and I miss him so much."

Danny carefully withdrew his hand from hers and

stood. "I'm glad you're remembering," he said. "I'll go call the doctor and let him know." He turned and started across the terrace toward the house.

"This is a wonderful day!" she said exuberantly. "Lots of good news."

Danny paused for a moment, turning to look at her. "Yes," he said, "lots of good news." But his expression was odd—remote, as if he were no longer involved in their conversation but merely a disinterested observer.

Her euphoria dropped a notch as he left the lanai. Sipping her juice, she thought back over their conversation. When she'd begun to tell him what she remembered, he disappeared. What had happened to cause that reaction? He'd withdrawn as surely as if he'd pulled a curtain down between them.

Leilani, the housekeeper who'd been so kind to her, came out to the table with a covered dish, which she set on a trivet with a conch-shell beside Sydney's plate. "Macadamia-nut pancakes, eggs Benedict and fresh pineapple," she said, whipping the shiny cover off with a flourish. "Guaranteed to put some meat on your skinny little bones."

Sydney forced a laugh, though her thoughts were still on Danny. "Thank you," she said. "Sounds delicious."

"Where Danny go?" Leilani asked, looking around.

Sydney shrugged. "I'm not sure."

Leilani made a plainly disgruntled sound beneath her breath. "Dat boy," she said, "need something to distract him from his troubles. But if he won't stick around and talk to you, how he gonna distract himself?"

Before Sydney could ask what she meant by that cryptic comment, the housekeeper had vanished, leaving her to eat her breakfast on the beautiful patio overlooking the ocean. From here she could see the green hills and red cliffs of Kauai, the island from which she'd come, and the marvelous blue shades of the water between.

What a beautiful spot to call your home. Of course, it was extremely isolated, which would never do for someone with children. Children needed other children to play with, places to go, things to see and try.

Suddenly, a reason for Danny's withdrawal occurred to her. Perhaps he thought she was married. He hadn't seemed to back away until she'd mentioned her son, she recalled. Could that be why? There was no denying that she found her host extremely attractive, and when he'd looked into her eyes she'd thought that perhaps he felt the same way.

It might have been nice to get to know him better.

Then she laughed at herself. *And how do you propose to do that, Sydney Leigh Ashton? The man lives on a remote Hawaiian island and you live in Portland.*

Thinking of Portland reminded her again of Nick. She hastened to finish her breakfast so she could call her mother in Washington and tell her that she wouldn't be home tomorrow as she'd originally planned.

But she wouldn't tell her mother about the boating

accident or what had possessed her to try to sail alone from Kauai to Nanilani. Or that she couldn't really remember much about Nicholas yet. She had the sense that there was something important, something urgent, that she still needed to recall, but it eluded her as surely as her name had eluded her for more than a day.

Oh, well. She finished her breakfast and gathered the dishes to carry inside so Leilani wouldn't have to make an extra trip out to get them. She'd just have to trust that it would come back, as everything else seemed to have.

And hope it was nothing terrible she was forgetting.

# Three

Sydney called her mother, who confessed she'd been getting worried. It wasn't like Sydney to go so long without calling, and she hadn't answered the phone in her hotel room.

After reassuring her mother, she spoke briefly to Nick. His grandfather had taken her son out on his tractor, and he was full of excited chatter about the big event. When she told him she'd probably be away a few more days, he didn't even protest. And although she sort of wished he missed her a little more, she knew that his easy acceptance was a good sign of a well-adjusted child. Given the nightmares he'd had off and on over the years—a recurrent dream in which someone was trying to steal him from her—she was particularly thankful.

Afterward, feeling ridiculously fatigued, she returned to the lovely room Leilani had put her in and took a nap.

She woke before noon, stretching and wincing when she began to move. Her shoulders, she'd noticed, were stiff and sore, presumably from something to do with the boat she'd been in or from swimming to shore. The ugly knot on her right temple was sore, too, as she'd discovered the hard way when she'd been washing her hair in the shower earlier.

As she rose from the bed, Leilani knocked quietly on the partially open door. "How you feelin' now, little miss?"

Sydney smiled. "Much better, thank you. I feel silly sleeping in the middle of the day. Usually it's my son who nods off."

"You have a son?"

At Sydney's nod, Leilani said, "How old?"

"He's five and a half."

The housekeeper's eyes widened. "The same age as Mr. Danny's little boy."

"Danny has a son, too? He hasn't mentioned him to me." She was too surprised to resist the urge to gossip, though she knew it was rude.

Leilani's expressive face was suddenly so sad that Sydney was alarmed. "What's wrong?"

"Mr. Danny's son kidnapped four years ago. Never been found."

"Dear heaven." Knees weak, Sydney reached for the edge of the mattress as she sank back down. "How old?"

"He was a year old when he was taken. He'd be five now, same as your little boy."

A shiver ran down Sydney's spine, making her shudder. "How awful."

"It is." Leilani shook her head sadly, then cleared her throat. "I didn't come up here to make you sad. I came to tell you lunch will be ready in about half an hour."

After Leilani had left the room, Sydney sat for a long moment on the edge of the bed. No wonder Danny had gotten quiet this morning. She had inadvertently reminded him of his pain, she was sure.

She couldn't even imagine what she'd do if something happened to Nick. His big blue eyes, the silky feel of his flyaway dark curls beneath her hand, the warmth of his small body snuggled against her when they read their nightly story… She could practically feel him in her arms right now and her throat grew tight. She missed him so much!

She wondered if his father— His father? A panicked sensation caught at her throat and tensed her muscles. She couldn't remember his father! Something was knocking at the closed doors of her consciousness, taunting her, but she simply couldn't bring it into focus. But it had something to do with her son, she was sure.

Why couldn't she remember his father? Her clasped

hands clenched so tightly her knuckles went white. It wasn't just the man she couldn't recall. There was absolutely nothing in her memory about Nick's birth. Or about the husband she must have had at the time. Was it possible she'd borne a child out of wedlock? She might have a head injury but she was pretty sure her moral values hadn't changed that much. Her instinctive recoil at the thought of giving a child the stigma of illegitimacy told her that it was highly unlikely she'd done so.

Thinking back over her conversation with her mother, she reflected that her mother had said nothing about her child's father. Was it possible there wasn't one in the picture? If that were true, where had he gone and why was she raising a child alone? Had he died? Surely she'd know it if he were dead.

She waited for some feeling, some sense of truth or falsehood to strike, but finally she had to admit that she had no idea, none at all, what the story of her son's father might be.

Darn it all! She'd had a few short moments of euphoria when she'd remembered her name and Nick and her family. She simply hadn't taken a complete mental inventory to see what else she might have lost that hadn't returned. She was so frustrated she could feel tears rising, and the weakness only made her angry, which made her cry even more.

Then she glanced at the clock and squeaked in alarm. Lunch was going to be served in a few moments. She didn't want to insult Leilani or her host by appearing rude or indifferent to their exceptional good-will. Springing to her feet, she rushed into the adjoining bathroom and splashed cold water over her face. Quickly she ran a brush through her shoulder-length brown hair, then headed for the terrace where Leilani had served breakfast.

Sydney rushed through the French doors onto the lanai breathlessly, saying "I'm sorry I'm late."

Danny turned from the edge of the flagstones, where he'd been standing studying the ocean. "Lunch hasn't been served yet."

Sydney made a nervous gesture, then caught herself and clasped her hands before her. The small movement made him wonder what she was so nervous about. "What have you been doing this morning?" he asked.

She smiled at that, a wry expression that made her lovely blue eyes twinkle. "I was busy napping. Breakfast wore me out."

"I'm not surprised."

"I think I must have been swimming before I hit the rock." She indicated her temple, where a striking blue-and-purple bruise had formed. "My shoulders are sore and my arms feel like two bags of concrete."

"Your boat hasn't washed up," he said. "Are you a strong swimmer?"

"I thought I was," she said. "I grew up swimming in a river with some pretty strong currents. But the current of Kauai's beaches was a shock the first day I got here."

He nodded. "There are a few places where it's protected and safe to swim. But there also are a lot of beaches that are too dangerous for swimmers. You should check at your hotel before going in the water."

Sydney smiled again. "Too late." Then the smile faded. "Although I might have asked. I don't remember. I don't remember getting a boat, either. I just have a vague impression of waves—one really big one—swamping a small boat I was in, and of swimming."

"Rogue wave," he told her. "It's not uncommon here for the surf to be unpredictable. An unusually large wave can come out of nowhere without any warning."

Leilani came onto the patio then with lunch, which she served beneath the same large umbrella where they'd eaten breakfast.

"This looks wonderful," Sydney told her. "What are these dishes?"

"Seared *ahi* with a mustard-soy sauce," Leilani said, "macadamia-nut wontons stuffed with brie, sea-vegetable salad and for dessert, Kilohana mud pie with mocha ice cream."

"*Ahi* is just tuna," Danny told her. "And she stole the recipe for the mud pie from her cousin who works at Gaylord's over on Kauai."

The housekeeper sniffed. "It was my idea first. She's the one who copied. But I don't mind. It's a compliment to know that my cooking is so in demand."

Danny couldn't entirely suppress the smile that tugged at his lips. "I bet you're making her pay you royalties on that recipe."

"Ha. What you know?" Leilani gave him her best menacing glare before turning and heading back into the house.

Sydney was staring at him. "Is she really mad at you?"

He shook his head. "Nah. She sharpens her tongue on me all the time. It's a good day when I can pay her back a little."

Sydney smiled at him as he stepped forward and held her chair. "She and her husband are sort of like family to you, aren't they?"

*Family.* The word actually hurt. He didn't know what to say, so he said nothing as he took his seat. But when he glanced at her, Sydney looked stricken.

"I'm so sorry," she said. "That was thoughtless of me. Leilani told me about your son."

He nodded curtly. "Apology accepted."

There was a strained silence as they passed the food. Sydney shook out a huge snowy white napkin and placed it over the short pink shirt and skirt set Leilani had given her that morning. The outfit was one that a granddaughter had left behind and it bared her pale, slender midriff and nicely toned arms.

Danny cleared his throat as she cut into her tuna. "If you'd like to tell me about your son, it's all right."

As olive branches went, he thought that was quite a large limb. Apparently she agreed, because she looked across the table at him. "He's just a typical little boy." Then she frowned. "Except for his family structure."

"What do you mean?"

"I'm not entirely sure," she admitted, frustration coloring her tone. "I thought I'd remembered everything but this morning I realized I can't recall anything about Nick's father. Nothing! It's like I found my baby under a toadstool or something."

"You mean you don't remember…" There was no way to put it delicately so he didn't finish the sentence.

A blush that matched her top flooded into her cheeks. "No. But it's odd. I don't feel as if I've ever been married, but I also don't think I'm the kind of woman who'd conceive a child without being in a committed relationship." She stumbled over her explanation a little, but plowed on. "I really don't have an idea what kind of person I am! I could have a much more colorful history than I think I do."

They ate in silence for a few minutes while he digested all that she'd told him.

"Have you asked anyone who knew you before?" he said at last. "About what you were like before this?" He didn't think she seemed like a woman who'd sleep around, either. She had the genteel, restrained manner of one who'd been raised a lady. She wasn't wearing a wedding ring and he'd bet she hadn't worn one any time in the recent past, because her ring finger was smooth and unmarred by any paler skin or slight groove from a ring.

"I talked to my mother briefly this morning," she told him, "but I didn't want to alarm her so I didn't tell her exactly what had happened. Also, I didn't realize until just a little while ago that there are still some gaps in my memory." Her voice rose in agitation. "Right now, all I want to do is go home and see Nicholas."

"I imagine you do," he said in an effort to calm her, "but it's only been a little more than a day since I found you. Eddie said you need to give yourself a couple of days to relax without any stress."

"It's stressful being away from my son," she said in an aggrieved tone. Then she seemed to realize what she had said. "I'm sorry." Her voice was much more subdued. "That's about as insensitive as I could get." She looked down at her plate.

"It's all right." He reached across the table and tapped the back of her hand gently. "I'm sure your son is in excellent hands with your mother. As for your memory lapse, why don't you try not to think about it for the rest of the day?"

Her wide brow wrinkled. "It's hard not to, when I'm just sitting around thinking, thinking, thinking all the time."

"Now, that I can help with." He withdrew his hand when he realized he was still lingering, tracing a finger over her soft, satiny skin. "After lunch, I'll take you down to the beach. It's beautiful. Then again, we're in Hawaii. Everything is beautiful."

"In its own way?" she asked immediately, the twinkle in her eye clueing him in to the fact that she was mimicking the words to an old tune.

He shook his head, groaning. "I'll only take you if you promise not to do that again."

Sydney smiled, and the small dimple in her left cheek winked at him. "I won't—if you don't give me the opportunity. My mother says I have a song for every occasion."

"My wife was like that," he said before he could stop himself.

She went still. "I didn't realize you'd been married." She made a face. "I guess I just didn't think about it or I'd have assumed you were."

"She's dead," he said before she could ask. "After Noah—my son—was kidnapped, she had a terrible struggle with depression. A year later she just couldn't deal with it anymore."

"She took her own life?" Sydney's eyes were soft and compassionate. "Oh, Danny, I'm so sorry. You've had some awful moments, haven't you?"

*You don't know the half of it,* he wanted to say. But he'd already talked too much about his problems. "If you're finished there," he pointed to her empty plate, "we can go down to the beach. Leilani's family has left every imaginable type of clothing here. I'm sure there's a bathing suit somewhere that will fit you."

"I'm not so certain I want to go swimming again," she said, and he could tell she was only half kidding.

"I wouldn't let you," he said seriously. "It's not safe to swim in the ocean at most of the beaches on Nanilani."

"Why?"

"Riptides that flow out through breaks in the reefs, really strong undertow, high surf a lot of the time—

you name it. But I'll show you some of the island's prettiest beaches and most unusual features."

"That sounds wonderful," she said, "but I'm not sure I'm up to hiking yet."

"You won't have to." He stood and came around to pull back her chair. "We use ATVs to get around the island."

While she went in search of a bathing suit, Danny brought one of the all-terrain vehicles around to the front of the house. It had a double seat to accommodate two passengers, and he put beach towels, water bottles, hats and sunscreen in the attached storage compartment. He also added reef shoes in sizes that he thought might fit her in case she wanted to walk in the water.

A few minutes later Sydney came out the door. She was wearing a sleeveless white T-shirt dress with armholes that drooped nearly to the waist, allowing him a glimpse of a powder-blue bikini beneath.

She climbed on the bike behind him, and Danny suddenly realized how intimate their excursion was going to be. "You'll have to put your arms around my waist and hang on," he said, clearing his throat. "I'm going to try to go slow and avoid the bumps so your head doesn't start to hurt again."

He climbed on the bike and waited for her to settle in behind him. His heart was racing and his body was far too aware of her slim frame as she got onto the bike. When her slender thighs were spread wide on either side of his and her hands gingerly clasped his waist, he thought he might expire with pleasure right on the spot.

He hadn't thought much about women since Felicia's death. He'd been functioning on autopilot for the first year or so after her suicide, but even in the three years after that, he hadn't cared about meeting anyone. He'd assumed his sex drive had died with Felicia.

But judging from the adrenaline rushing through his system now as he put the vehicle into gear and Sydney's small hands tightened around his waist, he'd been wrong in a big way.

Hell. Sydney was pretty, agreeable and sweet, and he hadn't been around a woman in ages. There was no more to his physical reaction than that.

He took the main path from the house down to the boat dock in the sheltered cove on the northeastern edge of the island. The reefs were larger and more plentiful all along the north beaches than on the south, and the small cove where the boats came in was a perfect spot to show her first.

He cut the engine and climbed off the bike, then helped her to stand. Her fingers clutched at his and he realized she was a little off-balance, so he slid an arm around her. "You okay?"

She gave him a wobbly smile. "Yes. Just a moment of dizziness. I don't know why."

*Swimming through God only knew what kind of surf and hitting your head on a rock might have something to do with it,* he could have said. But she knew that already. "This cove is where you'll come when you're ready to leave the island. Isn't it pretty?"

"It's beautiful," she said. He looked around, seeing it through her eyes. At the right side of the cove was the boat dock, where the water got deep a little faster than around the left side of the circular beach area. Several hundred yards offshore, the waves boiled up against the reef that protected the cove from the stronger surf.

"How do you get in and out of here? That looks dangerous." She was pointing in the direction he'd been looking.

"It is," he said. He dropped his arm and moved a pace away, a little unnerved how easy it felt to be with Sydney, to touch her as if they'd been touching for a long, long time. "But there's a big break in the reef around that headland to the right, and pilots who know the way in have no trouble. I don't usually swim here but it's possible over at the west end away from the currents."

He felt her actually shudder. "I don't think you have to worry about me swimming."

After they left Boat Cove, as it was known, he took her northwest around the island, following the beaches. "We have a lot more sand beaches here than the eastern islands do," he told her as they stood on a wide, sandy beach and watched breakers curl over an offshore reef. "Those islands are geologically a lot newer and haven't had time to build up the beaches or the reefs like this island has."

Danny shook out a blanket and sat down, stretching his legs and patting the place beside him. "Take a break. You probably could use a little rest."

"I hate to admit it, but you're right." She sat down a decorous distance from him, drawing up her knees and looping her arms around them as she gazed out to sea. "I've never been to Hawaii before," she said. "I had so much planned and here I sit on one little island, recuperating." She sighed.

A tingle of excitement that he hadn't felt in years shot through him. She was remembering more! Carefully, he said, "What kinds of things were you planning to do?"

"I wanted to see the Big Island while I was here," she said. "Get a close look at the volcanoes and maybe a lava flow. And I wanted to visit Pearl Harbor and tour the *Arizona* memorial on Oahu. It's all so beautiful, but I understand that each island is different."

He nodded. "Kauai has the distinction of having the wettest place on earth. The Big Island has Kilauea, the world's most active volcano. Each of the others has its own special something." He paused, then deliberately gave her a test. "Why did you start with Kauai?"

"I had to—" She stopped, whipped her head around to stare at him. "I remembered more, didn't I?"

He had to smile at her excitement. "You did."

"But…" Her obvious pleasure was fading fast. "When you asked me about Kauai, I got the strongest feeling that there was something I had to do here first. Something I had to finish before I went home." Her gaze grew unfocused, though no less intense. "But I can't remember what it was."

He put his hand on her shoulder and massaged, feeling the fragile joint, the smooth curve of her supple skin beneath his hand. "It'll come. Look at what just happened."

She sighed, an immense exhalation that shook her entire frame. "I hope so." She looked as pitiful as a balloon that had suddenly lost half its helium, and her misery affected him.

Pulling her close, he rubbed her back for a moment. "It'll come," he repeated. Maybe, he thought, he should hire a private detective. He could find out all about her life for her.

But Eddie had told him it was better if she remembered it for herself. And she'd already begun to recall her name, her family and major parts of her life. He'd wait awhile and see how much she got back before she was ready to leave. He'd prefer she remember and share it with him of her own free will.

He continued to stroke her back, enjoying the silky resiliency of her body beneath his palms as his pulse began to speed up. Sydney turned her face into his neck and laid her head against his shoulder, and her breath whispered across his skin. His breath caught in his throat and his heart stuttered. It would be so easy to draw her down onto the blanket they shared, to explore the feminine treasures of her body—

Whoa. What was he thinking? He was appalled at the intimacy he'd just created. They were alone on a deserted beach and he held her in his arms. A rogue wave of longing surged high and swept over him, urging him to drop his head and set his mouth against her soft pink lips. He wanted it so badly he actually felt his tense muscles shaking as he fought the need that had him tumbling in its rough surf. Releasing her, he surged to his feet. "Well. We should get going if you want to see the rest of the island's attractions."

Sydney was already gathering up the blanket and shaking out the sand. "Actually, I'm getting tired. It probably would be best if I went back and took a nap."

He was an idiot, he told himself as he pushed the ATV engine to its limits zipping up the steep hill to the house. Sydney's arms were snug around his waist, and he could feel the soft mounds of her breasts pressed against his back, the way the V of her thighs embraced him. He was appalled and fascinated with himself at the same time. He hadn't imagined he'd ever feel such a strong need to make love to a woman again. It was almost a relief to know his body still yearned for feminine contact, even though he and his right hand were perfectly capable of taking care of his needs himself.

But he didn't need Sydney, he reminded himself forcefully. He didn't need anyone, and the last thing he wanted was to be any more involved in her life than he already was.

# Four

She surely wished she knew what had happened down on the beach earlier, Sydney thought as she soaked in a bath of scented bubbles Leilani had produced from somewhere.

Danny Crosby was the most attractive man she'd ever met. She might not have all her memories but she was certain of that. When he'd hugged her, she'd known it was only meant as a gesture of comfort. But then the embrace had changed. She'd felt the quality of his caressing hands go from impersonal to something far more intimate, felt his body trembling against hers, felt him shudder when she'd given in to temptation and nuzzled her face into his neck.

She hadn't set out to tease him, she reassured herself. Whatever had happened had taken her as much by surprise as it apparently had Danny. But it had felt so *right.*

She wasn't one to ignore destiny, especially when it hit her over the head. As it literally nearly had.

Danny, on the other hand, clearly hadn't wanted to acknowledge the connection they'd shared. He'd held her for one all-too-brief moment and then he'd shot to his feet as though there was a rocket beneath his butt. He'd acted as if nothing of consequence had happened, and she'd followed his lead.

But she was fairly certain that he had been as aware of her as she had been of him. That wonderful feeling hadn't been all one-sided. She finished her bath and donned a short flowered robe. She hadn't been lying when she'd said she was tired, and she had just lain across the wide bed with her head cradled on her arms when someone knocked at the door.

"Come in." She rolled over and started to sit up, expecting Leilani. But it was Danny who entered as the door opened.

Sydney scrambled off the bed, mortified. The robe was short and she knew it hadn't been covering her bottom. All she had beneath it were the tiny bikini panties she'd been wearing when she'd washed up on the beach.

"Sorry." Danny sounded as embarrassed as she was.

"It's all right." She hated that she sounded breathless.

"I, uh, brought you something." He stepped into

the room and held up a suitcase, a purse and a small backpack.

"Oh!" She recognized them at once. "My things!" She was utterly delighted and touched by his thoughtfulness. "You got these from the hotel?"

He nodded. "No big deal. I thought you might like to have your own clothes. I checked you out so they wouldn't charge you for a room you weren't using, but they've promised to have a room for you when and if you decide to go back."

She tugged down the little flowered robe and crossed the room. "Thank you!"

"You're welcome." He handed her the purse and the small backpack but when she reached for the suitcase he didn't relinquish it. "This is heavy. Where would you like it?"

Her hand was snuggled up against his on the handle of the suitcase and his large body was close. Flustered, she stepped back and looked around the room. "Over there."

"Over there" was a wide upholstered bench just inside the doors to her small private terrace. Danny crossed the room and set the suitcase down.

Trailing him, Sydney placed the other bags beside it. "I guess I have a key somewhere," she said doubtfully, looking at the lock. "It's another one of those dopey little details that's still eluding me."

"Why don't you check before I go?" he suggested. "If not, I'll have Johnny open it. That man can do anything."

She smiled. She'd only met Leilani's husband once

but having seen the housekeeper in action, she wasn't surprised that her husband was equally capable.

Picking up the capacious shoulder bag, she unzipped the center pocket and peered inside. As the contents came into view, her memories of them came rushing back as well.

"Oh! I know exactly where it is." She dug into an inner side pocket and came up with a small brass key, then straightened and dangled it triumphantly in Danny's face. "See?"

Smiling down at her, he took her wrist and moved the key away from his nose. "That's great. So now you remember what's in there?"

She nodded. "And in there and there." Her smile faded a little. "I hope when I see Nick—my son—I remember everything else as easily."

"Like what?"

She shrugged. "I can see his face but it's like a painting. I can't hear his voice, and I don't know what he likes and dislikes. I can't really even recall how it feels to hold him."

Danny's fingers were still loosely circling her wrist, now down at her side. As he looked down at her, his eyes were very blue and very warm, although there was a shadow of sorrow deep in their depths that made her sorry she'd mentioned her son again. "It's coming back, piece by piece. You'll remember."

The utter certainty in his tone brought tears to her eyes. "Thank you," she said, fighting to keep her voice even. She put her free hand to his cheek. "I wouldn't

have been able to deal with this without your help."
She tried to smile. "They'd probably have me in a little padded room somewhere."

One of his rare smiles caught at the corner of his
lips. "I doubt that."

She couldn't hold back her own smile and for a moment they stood like that, just staring at each other. The
strong pull of intense attraction swept through her
again, and even as it registered, she saw an answering
need in his eyes.

Slowly, still holding his gaze, she moved her thumb
across the rough stubble of his jaw. Danny's free hand
came up and cradled hers, holding it there while he
turned his face into her palm. His eyes closed and she
felt the soft, moist touch of his lips against her palm.
Her body throbbed. She felt like a magnet being irre-
sistibly drawn to its opposite. *Kiss me,* her body whispered. *Touch me.* And as she swayed forward, she
knew that his body heard.

"Danny," she breathed.

His eyes opened and she felt him press the briefest
of kisses into her palm. Then he stepped back slowly,
letting her wrists slide free, and his eyes were no
longer a passionate electric blue, but a soft, sad color
that begged for her understanding. "I have to go," he
said quietly.

And before she could gather her scattered senses
and form a response, he was gone.

Shaking, she sank onto the edge of the bench holding her suitcase. She raised her palm and inspected it,

fully expecting to see scorch marks where his lips had touched her. No scorching. Slowly, she raised the hand to her mouth and touched her lips to the spot where his had rested. "Danny," she whispered again.

What did she want from him? It was hard to think rationally through the daze of sensuality that still held her in its grip. He made her practically limp with longing, and she knew without remembering so that she'd never felt the same way before. No man had ever made her knees wobble merely by touching her wrist or her palm.

She let her hand drop and it landed on her purse. Absently, she picked up the bag and set it in her lap. Distracted, she glanced down at it, and inside the open compartment saw her wallet.

Reaching in, she pulled out the small item and unsnapped it. Several photo sleeves ruffled as she did so and she slowly thumbed through them.

Nicholas. Her little Nick, in his soccer uniform, beaming. She remembered more now. He'd been so thrilled to play on the youngest of the youth league teams last year. In another he was much smaller, little more than a toddler, in a bright yellow and black bumblebee costume complete with tiny antennae on the hood. He carried a plastic pumpkin in one hand, preparing to go trick-or-treating. Several others were posed studio shots, in little bathing trunks on a simulated beach, all dressed up in what was clearly his Easter suit, sitting in pajamas in front of a Christmas fireplace scene.

He was adorable, and he was no longer a cardboard

cutout. She remembered his giggle, the way he'd had trouble saying *L*s—they came out *R*s when he was tiny—the clean smell of his freshly shampooed hair when he sat on her lap for his nightly story. But something…something was still missing, and it was driving her crazy. Whatever it was, it hovered right on the edge of her consciousness, but whenever she tried to bring it forward it shied away, back into the shadows. Why couldn't she remember every detail of her son's life? She knew the name of his preschool teacher but not his father. It was hard to imagine she'd been intimate with a man and now she couldn't even remember him. Could her son have been adopted?

An odd sense of panic swelled out of nowhere and she actually leaped to her feet, the purse and its contents spilling onto the floor. Thoroughly agitated, she knelt and began randomly gathering items and shoving them back into the bag.

What on earth was wrong? Her chest felt tight and she rubbed a hand over her breastbone, trying to make herself more comfortable. She'd been thinking about her son. Nick. Why would that upset her?

Making an effort to breathe deeply and relax, she opened the knapsack and larger suitcase and deliberately began to remove the items, stacking them neatly in the drawers of the dresser Leilani had told her she was welcome to use. Not that she'd had anything to put in it initially.

The simple actions calmed her more than anything, handling familiar items, savoring the memories associated with them. The flirty little sundress she'd shopped for with her mother before she'd left. The Portland Rose Festival T-shirt, the Oregon Zoo tank top from when she'd chaperoned Nick's preschool class, another T-shirt— Her fingers faltered as she saw the logo on it: Children's Connection.

Children's Connection was a nationally known fertility treatment center and adoption foundation that had started out years ago as a local orphanage and adoption agency. She knew that, could even picture the building's location, attached as it was to Portland General Hospital.

She couldn't explain the returning sense of unease, if not outright panic, that was crawling up her throat again. Hastily, she set the shirt in the drawer with the others and closed it, then put away several pairs of shorts and another sundress.

Danny had said her memory would return, she reminded herself as she took deep, slow breaths. And it had, in bits and pieces. The rest would come. She just had to be patient. Lucky for her, patience was one of her strengths. It had better be, because Danny Crosby was going to require a lot of it.

Thinking of Danny immediately distracted her. She was…awed by the feelings he awoke in her. There were unspoken wishes in his blue eyes that touched her deep inside, added to the undeniable physical pull they shared.

But what was she thinking? She had to go home. She had to hope she regained the rest of her memory.

She had to mother her son. Getting involved with Danny would be a bad, bad idea. He'd lost his best childhood friend and his own son to abductions. It was a bizarre coincidence, and enough to mess him up for life. Learning that his friend was alive after all these years had to be dredging up all kinds of feelings he'd probably iced over by now just to survive.

And then there was his wife. A tiny spark of anger flared within her. How could anyone think only of themselves in such a devastating situation? Hadn't the woman known how much Danny needed her? She was all he had left, and when she'd taken her own life she'd abandoned him. Rejected him, in a way. *You're not enough,* she'd said. Sydney was certain that if she'd been Danny's wife, she would have wanted to share the memories they had of their baby, to grieve and to hope and to fear together.

But she wasn't his wife. And it didn't matter how attracted she was to him, how compelling those blue eyes were, she couldn't get involved with him. He was a train wreck of emotional baggage that she knew she wasn't equipped for. Unquestionably, she should steer clear of Danny Crosby.

Danny stood on the terrace off his bedroom that evening and wished like hell he hadn't quit smoking. Maybe if he had something to do with his hands he wouldn't feel this jumpy, insistent need that Sydney Aston had aroused in him.

Until she'd come, he'd been happy. Okay, not

happy, but serene. Life was predictable and dull, exactly what he wanted after the tumultuous events that had followed him through childhood, into adolescence and ultimately even into his marriage. He never intended to care for another person again. Felicia had cured him of that. Not intentionally. He understood that she hadn't meant to harm him when she sat down in that bathtub and cut her wrists open. Her pain had been so raw, so overwhelming that she hadn't been able to see beyond it.

He'd been there and he could relate. Not that it made him feel any better. The bottom line was that Felicia hadn't cared for him enough to want to live. The bottom line was that he was done caring for people.

Oh, he still loved some of the members of his family, Katie and Ivy, and especially Trent, but he had no intention of adding to that list and risking yet another knife to the heart. How many times was a man expected to get stabbed before he died? How many could he survive?

He had a feeling he knew.

His resolve hardened. Getting any more involved with Sydney would be a huge mistake, for both of them. She needed, deserved a man who had a future. He was a man who hadn't survived the past.

Sydney had to go. She had to leave the island and she had to leave it soon.

To that end, he put in a call to Eddie Atada, asking him to come over tomorrow and examine Sydney again. If he found her well enough to travel, he, Danny, would pay for her transportation back to Kauai or one of the other islands if she preferred, until she was well enough to return to the mainland.

Eddie agreed to come over the following afternoon, and Danny knew a sense of relief. She could leave with Eddie tomorrow. He knew Leilani already had planned tonight's dinner, but it wouldn't be hard to pretend to be busy through the morning hours. Sydney didn't need to be entertained. Besides, if he told her what he intended, she would need to pack.

He thought he'd prepared himself, but when she walked onto the lanai before dinner, it was all he could do not to stare and slobber.

She wore a pale-blue fitted sweater and skirt in some silky material that clung to her slender frame in a way that the flowered robe hadn't. And though she'd worn a bikini earlier this morning, she'd also worn that baggy T-shirt dress as a cover-up so he really hadn't gotten a good look at her figure even then.

Now... He almost groaned aloud in sheer frustration. Now she looked utterly beautiful and intensely attractive. She'd acquired a little color from their time in the sun even though he'd insisted she be careful and use liberal quantities of sunscreen. The pale blue of the simple, clinging sweater and matching skirt made her skin look tanned and glowing, and gave a shining luster to her silvery blue eyes. Her arms and legs were bare, as was a generous amount of cleavage, and his fingers actually tingled with the need to touch all that flawless, lightly muscled skin. Her hair was nothing special, a no-frills brown in a straight, shoulder-length cut. But it gleamed with red highlights and swung in a perfect bell around her bare shoulders in the dying sunlight.

Danny closed his eyes for a moment. Maybe it was his imagination, maybe she didn't really look that good. But when he opened his eyes, her impact hadn't faded one bit.

Except for the expression on her face. When he'd first walked onto the terrace, her heart-shaped face had been warm with welcome. Now she looked puzzled, and increasingly concerned.

"Danny?" she said. "Are you all right?"

"Yeah." He cleared his throat, remembered the manners he'd learned from watching his brother Trent work a room at a business function. "Would you like a glass of wine?"

She nodded. "That would be lovely."

Good. That was good. He busied himself uncorking the wine and poured a glass for each of them. "So," he said, "do you work?"

She laughed, sounding startled. "Of course I work! I'm a campaign manager for a big public-relations firm."

He raised his eyebrows. "What firm?"

"Kremler, Dalhbright and Ackerman."

He nodded. "Crosby Systems has used them for a couple of things."

"I know." She smiled. "We got the account for the new client-presentation package three months ago."

"So you've probably met my brother, Trent."

She shrugged. "We've sat in a meeting or two. But his wife, Rebecca, is a friend, so yes, I've met him. I, uh, actually was at a bridal shower for them not long ago."

"He's a good guy," Danny said quietly.

"He's been good to Rebecca."

A silence fell. Danny wondered if she was feeling as awkward as he was. "Tell me about your childhood."

Sydney laughed. "Nothing earthshaking to tell. I grew up with an older brother and sister in a rural county outside Seattle. My mother was a teacher, my father was a plumber. They're both retired now. We got our first dog the year after I was born and he lived for fourteen years. We got our second dog, Bistro, the same year that Heath died and—"

"Bistro?"

She smiled wryly. "My sister was pretending she was a sophisticated cosmopolitan at the time."

"Ah. So what happened to Bistro?"

Her eyebrows rose in question. "Nothing. He's old and gray now but still tottering around after Mom." She took a breath. "We all went to the same schools and graduated from the same high school. My brother Stuart played football. Shelley and I were cheerleaders—"

"Stuart, Shelley and Sydney?"

She shrugged, a wry smile curving her lips. "My parents were on an S-streak, I guess. Anyway, I was a Student Council representative and I sang in the choir. Went to church every Sunday and helped with Bible school. And in the summer, my dad made us kids help weed the garden, which we thought was one of the subtlest forms of torture ever invented. I still can't stand peas after shelling bushels of them and helping my mother make split-pea soup for the church bazaar year after year." She laughed. "I've never served Nick split-pea soup in his life, but I bet he's been introduced to it by my mother this week."

Wow. She hadn't been kidding about the normalcy of her growing-up years. He could barely imagine such a blessedly mundane experience. In his house, his mother had always been screaming at one or the other of them, him more often than not.

"What about yours?"

He glanced up from the roast beef he was cutting. "My what?"

"Your childhood," she prompted.

He shook his head. "You don't really want to hear about my childhood, Sydney. There's nothing the least bit normal about it."

"I do." There was a quiet, unshakable determination in her tone.

He set down his fork. Very deliberately, he held her gaze across the table. "All right. My mother was an alcohol-sodden, self-centered bitch who should never have been allowed to breed. My father was a philanderer who found her so distasteful that he pretty much just distanced himself from the household. I was a lousy student. Anything else?"

Sydney didn't say a word. She just studied him, for

so long that he began to feel ashamed of his curt recital.

"I wonder why he married her," she said.

Danny uttered a bark of cynical laughter. "I've often asked myself that. I think she must have gotten pregnant, or else told him she was. A trick like that would be something she would do."

"You sound as if you're angry at her."

Danny shook his head. "Not angry, exactly. My past is like a bad dream. I do best if I don't think about it."

"But things are better now." There was certainty in her voice.

He hesitated, for some reason unwilling to be dishonest with her. "Not better, exactly. But…placid, I guess is a good way to describe life here."

The little dimple in her left cheek winked at him. "I refuse to believe you live here surrounded by all this beauty, where it never snows and almost always rains at night, and aren't happy."

He appreciated her attempt to lighten the mood. "I guess I am," he said. *As happy as I'm ever likely to be again.*

"You are," she said with certainty. "You know, I've never been anywhere outside the Pacific Northwest except for family vacations to Yellowstone, Niagara Falls and Disney World, in Florida, and a trip down the California coast, where we saw a whole lot of redwoods and wineries."

He had to chuckle. "Sounds memorable."

"Not when you're eight and you're stuck in the car for days on end. I always had to sit in the middle because Stuart and Shel would fight."

Again, he was struck by the utterly normal sound of her childhood memories.

"Did you fight with Trent?" she was asking.

He shook his head. "No."

"Are you close in age?"

He shrugged. "Three years, which is enough to make a difference when you're kids. And we hardly ever went to the same schools. My sisters were so much younger, I barely knew them."

"How many sisters do you have?"

"Two," he said. "Katie's six years younger than I am and Ivy's eight. I was sent away to school when they were still pretty young, so we never really had a chance to grow close."

Sydney's blue eyes were soft and sympathetic. "You were sent away?"

He nodded. "Yeah. Better educational opportunities, all that jazz."

"Did you like it?"

Did he like it? He debated telling her about the ridicule he'd endured from teachers who thought he was an easy mark because he wouldn't talk back, about the beatings for not making eye contact. About the freezing-cold showers and the weevils in the bread. About sleeping with a broken piece of metal bedrail because that was the only way he could protect himself from the older boys' abuse. He debated telling her that he didn't talk for eighteen months after Trent finally convinced their father, Jack, to get him out of there. "It was hell on earth," he finally said.

Sydney's eyes went wide. Apparently she'd discerned some of the truth from what he hadn't said. "It must have been," she said. "And you'd already been through so much."

"My parents didn't know what to do with me," he confessed before he could stop himself. "I was defiant, physically aggressive and getting completely out of control before I left."

"Were you always like that? Because you certainly aren't now."

He shook his head.

"So what hap— Oh."

"Yeah," he said. "Oh."

"How about counseling?" she suggested, her brows drawing together. "Did anyone ever offer you mental health help after your little friend was abducted?"

He uttered a short, harsh bark of amusement. "Yeah. That was right at the top of my mother's list, along with hugging her kids and doing volunteer work." His voice was loaded with sarcasm.

Sydney froze. He imagined she couldn't even conceive of a childhood as chaotic and frightening and lonely as his had been. Then she reached across the table and covered his hand with hers. "I'm so sorry, Danny. No child should ever have to endure all the things you did. It's a wonder you're still sane."

He almost told her *sane* was a relative state of mind. "I got past it," he said grimly.

"And then you lost your family." Were those tears pooling in her eyes? "How could you stand it?"

"I've learned to live with it," he said through his teeth. He really did not want to talk about this anymore.

"It's no wonder you've buried yourself in this quiet paradise."

"It's not a paradise," he said harshly, shoving back his chair and slamming away from the table. He shot her a look of bitterness, furious that she'd forced him to think about the royal screwup that was his whole life. "Don't you get it? It's a hideout."

# *Five*

*It's a hideout.*

There was a ringing silence in the wake of his explosion.

Danny stood with his back to Sydney, looking out over the low balustrade around the edge of the lanai. Beyond him, across the ocean, rose the cloud-shrouded peaks of Kauai. God, he wished he could just disappear into that thick mist. He felt as if one more word would shatter him like a plate of glass.

Sydney didn't say another word. But after a moment he heard her chair scrape back and her dainty footsteps cross the terrace to his side.

And then he went rigid with shock when her slim

arms slipped around his waist and she pressed herself to his back.

Holy heaven, but she felt good. Her breasts and thighs were soft against him, reminding him of how very long it had been since he'd known a woman's touch. Then he realized she was crying. Crying for *him*. And somehow it wasn't a turnoff but made him want her even more. More than the damn-near-constant wanting he'd known since she first opened those big blue eyes and blinked at him.

"I'm so sorry that I dredged all that up," she said, her voice breaking. "I only wanted to understand you a little better."

Hell. How could he stay mad after that? Her tears were soaking the back of his combed-cotton shirt and he could feel her body shaking with silent sobs.

"Hey," he said. With some difficulty he turned in the circle of her clinging arms, and now, sweet Lord, she was pressed against him from neck to knee, and her body flowed over the hard contours of his as if she'd been made to fit there exactly so. "It's all right." He put his own arms around her cautiously, overwhelmed by sensation and groping for the right words. "I'm sorry, too. I shouldn't have been so touchy."

"Yes, you should have." Her voice was muffled against his chest. "You've had some perfectly awful things happen in your life and I had to remind you of every single one of them."

"Sydney." He pried her away just enough to loosen her grip and place a finger beneath her chin, tipping her face up and forcing her to look at him. "It's okay. It's not like I ever forget, anyway."

"Never?" Her tears were slowing to an occasional sniff that hitched her breasts against him, making it even more difficult for him to keep his mind on the exchange.

He slowly shook his head. "Hardly ever. Except recently, sometimes…when I'm with you."

Her lovely, luminous eyes widened and suddenly there was an indefinable tension in the atmosphere that hadn't been there a second ago. He knew, without a word being spoken, that she was as aware of their intimate position as he was.

He wasn't going to kiss her, he insisted as her gaze fell to his mouth. Nope, he absolutely was not. But he lowered his head anyway, just for one breathless instant…

And then he was kissing her despite all his best intentions, her soft lips clinging to his, opening slightly when he traced them with his tongue, and finally opening wider to admit him as deeply as he could get. He slid his arms more fully around her, gathering her up against him, crushing her breasts against him, fitting his aching flesh to the soft notch between her thighs. The sensation was so exquisite that he groaned aloud as he changed the angle of the kiss and took her mouth again.

How long it had been… He couldn't sustain the thought, only knew that he hadn't felt like this in years. Maybe never. But he didn't want to think about the past, didn't want to think at all. Then Sydney shifted slightly, widening her stance enough that he moved even closer, enabling him now to feel the heat between her thighs. Ah, the heat.

She was like the lava that flowed down Kilauea's slopes, so hot she was burning him alive, twisting and turning, her mouth hot and passionate beneath his, her body pressed against him in surrender. He might not survive this, but he wasn't sure he cared. It was such a pleasure to feel passion again, to feel his body coming alive as it hadn't in a long time.

He tore his mouth from her and kissed his way down her neck, fiercely pleased when she shuddered and her head fell back. His fingers actually tingled with the need to experience her sweet flesh. He had to touch her or die, and he supported her with one arm while his other hand slipped beneath the little sleeveless sweater she wore, finding and stroking the smooth expanse of skin across her back and around her ribcage. His mouth moved lower, and her hands came up to thread through his hair and cradle his head as he found the swell of one breast and traced a path with his tongue along the lacy bra he discovered beneath her top.

At the same time, he slid a stealthy hand up beneath the bottom edge of the lingerie, cupping a surprisingly full breast and whisking his thumb over the already taut peak.

Sydney gasped. "Danny!"

"Sydney." His voice sounded strange, rough and

low. "Let me touch you." He tugged the sweater up and pushed the bra out of his way, and he actually heard himself make a noise deep in his throat as the perfect globe of one breast was exposed. Her nipple was a deep rose, standing up tight and proud, and he bent his head to her, running his tongue around the tip and then sucking at her. His body was the one on fire now, and he shifted uncomfortably in the suddenly too-tight khaki trousers he'd worn to dinner.

He wanted her, wanted her so badly that his thoughts were swirling around in his head like high waves around a reef. "I want you," he murmured, lifting his mouth a fraction. "Come upstairs with me."

"What?" She sounded dazed and bewildered.

"I want you in my bed," he said, kissing her breast again.

Sydney's body, which had been so pliant and fluid against his, suddenly stiffened. Her hands fell away from his hair and she began to push at his shoulders. "Wait, Danny," she said. "Stop. Please."

He felt like a person coming out of a deep, deep sleep. Disoriented and confused. It was a long moment before the words penetrated the sexual haze into which he'd fallen. But finally, her lack of response got through. He lifted his head and saw indecision on her passion-flushed face. It was quickly replaced by a growing wariness that stung. Surely she knew she didn't have to be afraid of him, didn't she? He immediately released her, taking a moment to pull her top back into place. Silently mourning the loss of both the sight and sensations of her, he stepped a pace away, turning his back and staring blindly out over the ocean. His current condition was a little embarrassing, not to mention sure to make both of them doubly uncomfortable.

Behind him, she said, "I'm sorry, Danny. I should never have let that go so far."

No response was required so he didn't say anything.

Sydney cleared her throat. "I'd better, uh, just go on up." Again she hesitated. "It's not you, Danny. I don't want you to think that I'm not attracted to you. But I have to think about my son. What kind of mother would I be if I was willing to hop into bed with a man I've only known a couple of days?"

He could understand that rationale, could even applaud it with the part of his mind that wasn't occupied trying to will away his raging arousal. "Go, Sydney," he said. "I'm not stopping you."

She stood there for another long moment, but finally, to his intense relief, he heard her soft footfalls turn away and walk into the house.

It was for the best, he assured himself. Sleeping with an uninvited, temporary guest would have been a huge mistake. It didn't matter. He couldn't let it matter that she was the first person he'd woken up anticipating seeing in a long, long time.

Tomorrow the doc could take her back to Kauai and get her settled somewhere there until she felt able to travel home again.

* * *

She must be an early riser, because when he went down to breakfast after finishing his morning workout and showering, Sydney was already seated at the table on the lanai. She appeared to be done eating and when he said, "Good morning," she glanced up and smiled, a brief, impersonal change of expression that meant nothing.

"Good morning."

Then she rose, avoiding his gaze, and he realized she was going to leave him to dine alone. He almost protested but then remembered last night. The less time he spent with her, the less he would mind it when he was alone again. Still, he would be a poor host if he didn't check on her health, given the manner in which she'd arrived. "Sydney, wait a minute."

She stopped and turned.

"How are you feeling?"

She shrugged. "Fine. Still stiff and sore, but that will pass."

He shook his head. "I mean, how are you doing? Have you remembered anything else?"

She nodded. "Some things. I can picture my office and the people I work with, my family, my child-hood...but I still have the sense that I'm missing something important." She shook her head. "But I can't imagine what it could be, because there aren't many glaring gaps in my memories now."

He noticed she didn't say there weren't *any*. "That's good," he said aloud. "I, uh, spoke with Dr. Atada. He's coming over at three to check you out again. Then he's going to take you back to Kauai, to a hotel, until you're ready to fly home. It'll be better if you're somewhere close so that the doctor can keep an eye on you." He realized he was babbling nervously and he clamped his mouth shut.

Sydney's eyes had gone very wide at first, then she simply seemed to deflate. "All right," she said quietly. "I'll go and gather my things."

Oddly enough, he felt almost annoyed at her easy acquiescence. "Do you remember how long you initially planned to vacation?" he asked.

She hesitated, then nodded. "A week. And I've already spent two additional days recuperating." Her eyes were sad. "Thank you for your hospitality. Even if I never remember everything, it'll be nice to have memories of such a lovely place. I'm just sorry I didn't get to see more of Hawaii."

Before he could talk himself out of the impulsive offer, Danny said, "I can't offer you Oahu and the Big Island all in one day, but how would you like to take a helicopter tour before you leave? We can see Nani-lani, Kauai and Ni'ihau from the air." It was just guilt, he decided, because he felt as if he was kicking her out. It wasn't that he particularly wanted to spend more time in her company.

Of course not.

But Sydney was shaking her head. "Oh, no thank you. It's a generous offer, but I couldn't possibly…." Her cheeks were growing pink. "I wasn't complaining—"

"Sydney."

She shut her mouth abruptly and simply looked at him.

"I wouldn't have offered if I didn't mean it. In fact, I think I'll go whether or not you do. I've never taken an air tour, either."

"You haven't? But you live here!" There was astonishment in her voice.

"That's right. I live *here*. I haven't had the urge to leave or do much of anything."

Her brow furrowed. "Danny, exactly how long is it since you've been off this island?"

He smiled. "I've spent almost four years here without setting foot off this place."

"You mean four years since you left Hawaii," she said doubtfully.

He shook his head. "Four years since I left this island."

She looked shocked. But he didn't really want to pursue the topic, so as she opened her mouth again he said, "So what do you think? Would you like to go on a tour?"

She nodded. "Yes, but only if you're not just doing it because you feel sorry for me."

"I don't feel sorry for you," he said.

"But won't it be difficult to line up a tour on such short notice?" she asked. "I thought those helicopter tours had to be booked well in advance."

"Not always. I'll go talk to Leilani and see if I can make it happen." As he walked into the house, he realized Sydney didn't really have a concept of just how much money he had. Did she know he could buy a whole helicopter fleet today if he felt like it?

He'd never felt particularly privileged, though he knew most people looking at his life from the surface would trade places with him in a heartbeat. So many people believed money would make them happy.

Those people, though, had never spent their childhoods believing they were responsible for a tragedy. Those people hadn't grown up with a mother who was far more in love with a booze bottle and searching for her own pleasure than she was in raising or reassuring her children. Those people hadn't been shuffled off to military school "for their own good." And he was damn sure none of those people had had a son abducted and a wife commit suicide.

No, money couldn't buy happiness. And he was pretty damn certain that if he had a lot less of it he would still be the same guy who'd withdrawn from the world. He might be living under a bridge somewhere instead of on an island in the Pacific, but would he really care?

Probably not.

Thirty minutes later he knocked on the door of Sydney's bedroom.

The sound of light footsteps crossing the floor caught his ear, then the knob turned. "Hello," Sydney said.

"Ready to go for a ride?" he asked.

Her face lit up as if someone had touched a match to a waiting wick. "Are you kidding? I never thought you'd be able to arrange it!"

Her open delight warmed him. It had been a long time since he'd seen anyone smile at him like that. "He'll be here in about ten minutes. You might want to tie your hair back or something."

"I'll braid it," she said. Turning around, she rushed to the low vanity and tossed open the lid of a small travel case. She rummaged around and finally came up with a comb and a fat elastic band. "Give me two minutes," she said.

He could have left. *Should* have left. But as Sydney turned back to the mirror and her fingers began to weave her hair, he simply stood in the doorway and drank in the sight.

Her fingers flew, separating and gathering small sections of hair, braiding it into a single smooth line starting at the crown of her head. She'd lifted her arms above her head and the motion pulled her shirt taut against the lower curves of small, pert breasts. Her arms were graceful curves, the whole picture so quintessentially feminine that Danny found himself battling the urge to cross the room and put his arms around her.

Her hair was shoulder-length and by the time she got to the nape of her neck, there were no more loose strands. Deftly, she twisted the elastic around the bottom of the braid several times until it was tight.

She dropped the comb and turned around again. "There," she said. "Less than two minutes."

"You're, uh, good at that," he said, and had to clear his throat. He'd thought she was pretty before, but with all her hair back away from her face, the smooth, oval perfection of her patrician features was revealed. Wide blue eyes beneath finely arched brows, a small straight nose and the full bow of her lips. High cheekbones that emphasized the fragility of her face.

"Lots of practice." She smiled at him, and the expression crinkled her eyes and invited him to share in her amusement. She turned and picked up a small backpack-style bag, which she slung over one shoulder. "Okay. I'm ready."

She'd never thought about how loud a helicopter flight would be. Fortunately, the pilot Danny had engaged had three headsets that muffled the noise even as it permitted him to talk about the geographical wonders over which they flew.

After a quick pass over the tiny bulk of Nanilani, with its black cliffs and golden sand beaches, the pilot flew west, over the privately owned island of Ni'ihau. A shield volcano had erupted there once, the pilot informed them, and much of the wider northern end of the heavily forested, sparsely populated island was formed by low-rise cinder cones and lava flows. All the western islands, he explained, were no longer part of the active volcanic region. Far older than the young, fiery islands to the southeast, Ni'ihau, Kauai and Nanilani were actually in the slow process of eroding back into the sea from which they'd been born. The string

of tiny islands that could be seen stretching even farther west, including Midway and the Pearl and Her-
mes atolls, names she recognized from her high-school
history class, were even farther along in the process of
being cannibalized by the ocean.

The pilot didn't spend much time on Ni'ihau before
heading due north for a flyby of a tiny islet, Lehua
Rock. Looking like a giant crab claw, Lehua's sea-
breached semicircle was all that remained of a volcanic crater from ages past. It was both fascinating and
utterly alien.

After Lehua, the plane veered east toward Kauai.
As the cottony puffs of clouds receded and Kauai came
into full view, she caught her breath. The island was
lovely. The corner of her eye spotted a movement and
she turned to meet Danny's eyes.

*Wow,* he mouthed, and she grinned, nodding her
head. Wow, indeed. And not just wow to the air tour,
she thought. Every time she met Danny's intense blue
eyes, she felt a little *zing* of recognition or attraction.
And if she were honest, arousal as well. The man was
so gorgeous he made her want to pant. And that kiss…
An involuntary shiver chased itself down her spine.
She could spend the rest of her life kissing Danny
Crosby. Among other things.

Ah. Other things. Besides recalling the fact that she
wasn't married, had never been, she'd given little
thought to her level of experience with the opposite
sex. But now she realized that she also knew she
wasn't a virgin.

Oh, she wasn't a slut, but she hadn't had much sexual experience. Just one semi-serious relationship in college with... She waited for the memory to reform. Micah. That had been his name. She'd thought for a while she might be in love with him, but they'd drifted apart after graduation with no rancor and even less desire to put in the work necessary to maintain a relationship.

Since then, she'd dated steadily but not seriously. Or at least she had until her son came along—

The thought stopped her abruptly. That one gaping hole still left in her memory was making her far more uneasy than it should. Why couldn't she remember Nick's birth? Had he been adopted, as she was beginning to suspect? And if so, why would she have chosen to adopt a child as a young single woman? There was something...something just beyond her reach that was important. Or at least she thought so.

She wished she knew the whole story so she could share it with Danny. They were crossing a short stretch of ocean between Lehua and Kauai now, and she turned and glanced at the object of her thoughts.

He was watching her.

That simple meeting of their eyes doubled her heartbeat but she forced herself to ignore it. She smiled at him, indicated the window where the islands and whitecaps lay beneath them and mouthed, "Thank you."

He smiled back and the expression lit his face with extraordinary charm. He didn't smile often, but usually was sober and hard to read, his handsome features set in granite. But oh, when he smiled... It transformed his handsome features. His blue eyes danced, and her foolish heart was sure there was a special softness hidden there meant just for her.

Then he reached over and took her hand where it lay on the armrest of the seat. Raising it to his lips, he pressed a gentle kiss to the back of it as he watched her steadily.

She had to close her eyes for a second when the warmth of his mouth touched her skin. Desire, bright and blinding, rose in a rush, urging her to unbuckle her seatbelt and climb right over there into his lap.

But it didn't matter, she reminded herself. She'd be leaving later in the day, and although he'd been a most gracious host, she knew she would never see him again. His eyes might tell her that he wished things were different, but Danny wrapped his isolation around himself like a blanket holding the chill at bay. And now that she understood all the harrowing experiences that had shaped his life, she had to respect his decision to keep his life placid, pleasant—and utterly devoid of any emotional entanglement.

The pilot spoke again and she returned her attention to the view beyond their flying bubble. Kauai, he said, had forty-three beaches strung around it, more per mile than any of the other six major islands. Its western coast lay before them, the fifteen-mile stretch of sand beaches pounded by some of the most treacherous surf on the island. The beaches were generally sun-kissed and beautiful, although along the wild and inaccessible coastline there, they were rarely visited. It was easy to see why, as the helicopter flew over verdant, two-thousand-foot-high cliffs that had been so heavily eroded they reminded her of the fluted edges of a pie crust or a rumpled blanket. Their name, the Na Pali range, meant cliffs in Hawaiian.

While the coastal areas were quite dry, she was astonished to learn that the peak of Wai'ale'ale, visible in the middle of the island, bore the distinction of being the wettest spot on Earth. As they continued eastward, her mouth suddenly fell open. They were flying over a deep, heavily eroded canyon that reminded her strongly of Arizona's Grand Canyon. She pointed down, raising her eyebrows at Danny questioningly. He shot her another grin, accompanied by a "don't ask me" shrug of his shoulders, and she felt that funny little hitch in her heartbeat again.

Their pilot had caught her gesture. They were over Waimea Canyon, he explained. He pointed out a rainbow shimmering in the mist to their right, and then took them down for an adrenaline thrill as they appeared to maneuver almost between some of the jutting peaks.

She was enchanted. Waterfalls spouted from the cliff walls and fell to the valley floor. And though they continued on around Kauai, nothing else she saw could compare to the wild, romantic appeal of the canyon.

A lot like her host.

She was very much afraid that no matter how many

men she met after she returned home, none of them would touch her heart or draw her body's response like the lonely, unexpectedly irresistible man she'd found on a small, isolated island.

## Six

Danny was quiet once they were back on the ground. She'd thanked him effusively after they'd climbed out of the helicopter, and she thought perhaps she'd embarrassed him.

Or maybe he just couldn't wait to get rid of her. She checked the clock on the hall table. Dr. Atada would be arriving at three to take her back to Kauai. She should just go on up and get her things. A short and sweet leave-taking would definitely be for the best, she thought, an ache in her throat.

But as she turned toward the stairs, Danny caught her elbow. "Sydney, I—"

"Thank you again," she said quickly. "I'll go bring down my bags."

"I asked Johnny to bring down your suitcase," he told her. "Leilani made us a late lunch on the lanai. Would you like to have one last meal here before you go?"

Sydney stared up at him, trying to read his expression. He was a confusing mass of contradictions. One minute she'd swear he couldn't wait to get rid of her, the next he seemed to be begging for her company. She could only hope that meant she sent him into the same kind of tailspin that his presence had done to her.

*It doesn't matter,* she reminded herself fiercely. Aloud, she said, "That sounds lovely. Thank you."

The meal was as beautifully presented and unique as always. Danny informed her it was called lomi salmon, a chilled salad mix of raw, salted salmon, tomatoes and onions. Leilani had asked her yesterday if she liked sushi, and Sydney now realized why she'd asked. The salad was delicious. For dessert, there was a Jell-O ring studded with Methley plums, a local delicacy harvested at Kohe'e State Park.

As Leilani carefully placed the dessert mold on the table after clearing their lunch plates, the Jell-O wiggled lightly. Sydney turned her head to look fully at it—

And was stunned by a vivid wave of memory bursting through her like the sea through a hole in a boat.

The ring in the middle of the Jell-O…a hole in a boat… *Her* boat!

"Danny," she blurted. "I know how I got here."

He looked at her, clearly interested. "You remember it?"

She nodded. "I just did. It was the Jell-O." Her voice trailed away as the import of all the memories racing through her fully registered. Dear God. Danny—

His voice intruded. "Sydney, what's wrong? What are you recalling?" He laid his hand over her suddenly chilled fingers and squeezed lightly.

"Oh, Danny," she said miserably, "I know why I wanted to see where you live, and why I wanted to meet you. I rented a speedboat. It took me almost all day to find someone who would let me take a boat out alone—"

"And he shouldn't have," Danny said grimly. "The ocean is vastly different from anything you were used to before."

She nodded. "I got caught in a strong current and carried onto the reef just offshore. The coral tore a hole in the boat and it went down so fast…. One moment I was wrestling with the motor, the next I was in the water."

"You're incredibly lucky," he said, his voice harsh. "You could have been ripped to shreds on that coral, or swept right on past the island into one of the Pacific currents." He stopped abruptly, his tone altering. "You wanted to meet me?"

Too late, she realized this wasn't the way to tell him. But she'd been so shaken by the return of the memories she'd just blurted it out. Her throat was so tight she couldn't speak, and she just stared at him, wondering how to tell him why she'd come.

"Sydney," he said in an implacable tone. "How did you know my name and why was it so important to see where I lived that you took a chance with your life like that?"

She cleared her throat. Quietly, she said, "I didn't intend to contact you this way. But I had hoped to meet with you while I was in Hawaii." She squared her shoulders and took a deep breath, wondering how she was going to live with the hurt her suspicions would bring. "Danny...I believe my adopted son, Nicholas, is your Noah."

He couldn't believe his ears. He'd thought she was so special, had been so attracted to her. And all the time she was nothing but a fortune hunter. Fury rose, swift and boiling. "And let me guess," he said with heavy sarcasm. "For the small sum of what? One million? Two? You'll let me have him without a court battle? Or has the price gone up in the past couple of years?" He pushed back his chair so abruptly it crashed backward onto the stone floor of the lanai. "You don't honestly think you're the first person who's tried to hoodwink me with a fake kid, do you?" He laughed, a bark of sound devoid of any humor. "You know, the first time—hell, even the second—I believed it. I wanted Noah back so badly that I'd have believed anything. But after the fifth time I'd gotten pretty wise to the tricks. Just goes to show I've been hiding away too long since I didn't recognize you for what you were."

"Danny, no," she said, a quaver in her voice, and he

steeled his heart against the plea in her soft eyes. "I don't want your money."

"Right."

"I don't!" She sounded a little indignant now. Playing it just right, he thought bitterly. "All I want is for you to take a DNA test that will prove whether or not my suspicions are correct." Her voice hitched and she paused, pressing the back of her hand against her mouth for a moment until she'd regained control. "I couldn't live with myself if I denied my son the chance to be reunited with his real father." Her voice dropped. "And you with your son."

No. She was lying. She might be pretending she didn't want money, but she'd change her tune once she thought she'd hooked him into believing her. They all did. Noah was dead, had probably been dead for several years by now. Without the heart surgery he'd needed, he wouldn't have stood a chance.

Pain he thought he'd managed to shut in a forgotten box seared him and he actually reached out for the door frame to steady himself. He couldn't look at Sydney anymore.

"You won't be going to Kauai this afternoon," he informed her.

Behind him, she said, "I won't?" in a startled voice.

"You're not going anywhere until the police talk to you."

"Please," Leslie Logan said. "We want to know everything you can find out about his past. His parents.

Any other family. His childhood, what schools he attended, who his friends were…" She bit her lip fiercely as her eyes welled with tears.

Terrence Logan put one arm around his wife's shaking shoulders. "Can you help us?" he asked the private investigator.

The man shrugged. "I can try. But there are no guarantees in this kind of work."

"We understand that," Terrence said.

"Now tell me everything you know about this…" He consulted his notes. "Everett Baker."

"He was an employee of Children's Connection, the adoption and infertility treatment program that's been our special project for years," Terrence said. "He was arrested for kidnapping babies and adopting them out to wealthy people for astronomical sums of money."

"You already know our firstborn son was abducted at the age of six. About a year later we were told his body had been found. Now we learn that our son didn't die." Leslie carefully dabbed beneath her eyes one final time, then straightened her shoulders.

"And this Baker says he's your son?" the P.I. asked.

Terrence nodded.

"I know what you're thinking." Leslie leaned forward. "Fortune hunter, right? But we're already convinced he's our son, based on things he's spoken of that no one else could possibly have known. We simply want you to fill in the blanks."

"Why don't you just ask him to take a DNA test?"

"We will," Leslie said, "but we want to know more about him before we discuss that."

"He's been accused of a crime," Terrence said bluntly. "And we don't believe he would willingly have done the things he's accused of without someone else leading him on. We need information because we plan to provide for Robbie—for Everett's defense."

"I'll have to check your information," the investigator said almost apologetically. "I'll only take on the case if I believe you have a legitimate reason for wanting information about this young man." He grimaced. "I've had too many enraged spouses in my office wanting background on someone for the sole purpose of harming them in some way."

Terrence nearly smiled. "We appreciate ethical convictions. That only convinces me you're the right person for the job."

"Our lives are an open book," Leslie said. "Would you like us to give you the names of people you can talk with about us?"

The man nodded. "That would be helpful, Mrs. Logan."

Leslie stood and went to an elegant mahogany desk along one wall of the sitting room in which they'd met with the investigator. She returned with a notepad as well as a slim file folder, which she handed to the man. "This is everything we know about our son's past, both before and after he was abducted." She sat again and took several moments to write on the notepad she held. Tearing off the top sheet, she extended it to him. "These are people you can call for references on us as well as for any more information on the original investigation. The first name is the retired police chief who handled the abduction when it occurred. The second is the general number for Children's Connection. People there knew Everett Baker. They also know us and you can speak with anyone there you like. The last three numbers are our family physician and two longtime friends. Our children's names—our other children's names— and numbers are already in the folder, in case you should need to speak with them. But they're all younger than Robbie. None of them even knew him." Her lip quivered again but she took a deep breath and bit into her lip. After a moment, her lovely features relaxed again.

The private investigator stood, sliding the loose note into the folder as he extended his hand first to Terrence and then to Leslie. "I expect that will be a formality, Mr. and Mrs. Logan. I'll be in touch within the week to let you know how the investigation is going."

"Thank you," Terrence said.

"Yes, thank you," Leslie echoed. "You can't imagine what it means to us to learn that our son is living." A smile lightened the sorrow in her eyes. "After all these years…it's a miracle."

"Then I'll do my best to ensure that your miracle stays out of prison," the P.I. said.

Within an hour, Danny's lawyer and the police chief had arrived. Danny and the chief watched through a hastily set up video feed while Danny's lawyer questioned Sydney. She'd agreed to answer the man's questions without any hesitation. She'd even asked Danny if he wanted to listen, and had looked disappointed and unhappy when he'd refused. Oh, she was good. No doubt about it.

"Tell me why you think your son is Noah Crosby, Ms. Aston. You say you got him under questionable circumstances?"

"It's Miss," Sydney said quietly. She linked her fingers in her lap. "Four years ago, in January of 2001, I received a call from a woman who'd been a friend— an acquaintance, really—from college. She said she'd gotten my name from another friend and wanted to visit while she was in Seattle. That's where I was living at the time."

The lawyer made an encouraging noise, and Sydney went on. "When she arrived, she had her son with her. She said he was about a year old, but she was evasive about his birthday. Also, I remember thinking that she and the child didn't seem bonded. The baby didn't seem to find her particularly comforting, didn't look for her or hold up his arms when she came near. It was...odd. But at the time, it didn't seem significant. Margo, my friend, looked bad. Her clothes weren't especially clean and she had a bruise down the side of her face and several more on her arms that she tried to keep covered. She was dead broke and if I had turned her away she would have had to go to a shelter. So I let them stay with me. Eventually Margo confided in me. She said the baby's name was Nicholas—Nick—and that his father was dead. She said the bruises were from a boyfriend who'd gotten abusive. I think his name was Charlie or Chuck, something like that. I'm afraid I don't really remember."

"It's all right. Go on."

"They stayed with me for three weeks and I adored little Nick. He seemed to like me, too, and I told Margo she could stay as long as she needed. But one day when I got home from work, Margo was gone. Nick was alone in my apartment in the crib I'd bought, screaming his poor little head off." She took a deep breath. "On the floor by the bed was a paper bag and in the bag...in the bag was one hundred thousand dollars. In cash!" She sounded sincerely shocked. After a moment, she gathered herself again.

"I put the money in the bank and got a neighbor to baby-sit during the day. I was sure Margo would be back soon. Who in the world walks away from a precious child like that?"

*Not to mention the money,* Danny thought. But Sydney never said another word about it.

"One day, when she'd been gone for a little more than three weeks, I saw on the news that they'd found a woman's body caught on some branches in a stream in the mountains outside Seattle." She put a hand to her throat and Danny could see horror on her face. "They identified her through dental records. It was Margo."

"The baby's mother." The attorney wore no expression as he listened.

".Yes. Or so I believed at the time." She unclasped and relaced her fingers in the first sign of nerves she'd shown.

Maybe the first part of the story was true, Danny thought. She sure hadn't sounded like she was lying. But the lies were about to begin. This was where she would claim Nick was really his Noah.

"I called Social Services and applied to become his temporary foster home, which they granted. They tried to find family, both the mother's and the father's, but no one ever came forward, so after going through a lengthy adoption process that lasted over a year, I adopted Nicholas. And shortly after that we moved to Portland because I got a good job offer there."

"And the money the woman left?"

"I put it in a trust for Nicholas. It's in care of a local bank until he turns eighteen. I couldn't access it if I wanted."

The lawyer let a silence hang. After a moment, he said, "Miss Aston, why do you think your son is Noah Crosby?"

Danny closed his eyes for a moment. God, it still hurt so badly.

"Nick has had nightmares," she said, "from the time he was an infant. Every once in a while he wakes up screaming."

"I'm no expert," said Danny's lawyer, "but don't a lot of children do that occasionally? Mine did."

"This is different," she said in the same patient tone she'd employed all along. Why wasn't she angry at this interrogation, Danny wondered. "Margo had told me Nick was about a year old so I chose a January birth date. By his third birthday, he could articulate his dreams. It's always the same dream. Over and over. As he's grown older, he's continued to describe the dream, and it's still always the same. Someone is stealing him. Now, of course, someone is stealing him from me, which obviously wouldn't have been the case four years ago, but the basic dream is the same."

"Have you ever consulted anyone about these dreams?"

"Dream," she corrected. "One dream, many times over. And the answer is yes. After we moved to Portland I joined a group called the Parents Adoption Network. After several months I mentioned the dream. Most people had your reaction, but one mother took me aside later and told me that if it were her child, she'd be concerned, too, that what I described wasn't normal. So I took him to a child psychologist, whom we're still seeing. The dream hasn't changed, but he's been having fewer nightmares recently."

"That still doesn't explain why you think your child is Mr. Crosby's son."

"Timing," Sydney said. "I only became aware of the traffic in stolen infants after I joined PAN. A few months ago, Nick's counselor told me the fact that Nick had the same dream over and over might be significant. Of course, I immediately wondered if he was a stolen baby. I did some research on children who had been stolen within the year before I got Nick. The time frame of Noah Crosby's kidnapping fits most closely within the Pacific Northwest. The only other one that matches the time frame, assuming Nick hadn't been with Margo very long, was a child taken in Georgia, and that was a newborn. I think this might explain why Nick didn't seem attached to Margo when they first arrived. And there was something else: I told you how odd I thought it was that Margo didn't seem especially good at calming her child. He screamed a lot at first and seemed to have a lot of gastric distress. Margo said it was just gas, but after I became his foster mother, I took him to a doctor who diagnosed him as severely lactose intolerant. Looking back, I don't believe Margo knew it."

Danny caught his breath and his heart leaped. His son, Noah, had been lactose intolerant. Felicia had also been allergic to dairy products. She hadn't even been able to eat a slice of their wedding cake because of the milk content in the recipe and the butter in the frosting. Noah had inherited it. He'd even had a reaction to Felicia's breast milk and they'd had to put him on soy formula.

It was one of the things they'd agonized about after the kidnapping. That and the heart defect.

Still, this could just be coincidence, he assured himself. Nick Aston wasn't his son. Noah was as dead as Felicia. For a long time he'd hoped…but that hope had been futile. He had no intention of destroying himself on that emotional roller coaster again.

On the screen, the lawyer was thanking Sydney,

who got up and left the room. He turned to face the camera, shaking his head. "I don't know, Danny," he said. "My gut feeling is that she's not lying. Not about any of it. I suspect she'd take a polygraph if you asked her to. And of course there's DNA testing."

There was no need for DNA testing. None at all. *Nicholas Aston was not his son!* He forced himself to take deep, calming breaths, but he could feel his whole body trembling with the anxiety that had risen again. Dammit! He could not afford to do this again, he thought wearily. He glanced at the cop seated beside him. "So?"

The chief had listened impassively to Sydney's story and the lawyer's subsequent comments. He looked at Danny and then sighed. "What, exactly, do you want me to do? The young lady washed up on a public beach and you invited her to stay in your home. It's true that she did it under false pretenses, but it sounds as if the way she contacted you was a genuine accident. And Dr. Atada said he didn't think she was faking the memory loss. In any case, that's not a crime. And she swears she doesn't want money from you, so I can't charge her with attempted extortion."

Danny raked his fingers through his hair. Despite his agony, he'd suspected the chief couldn't do much of anything to Sydney. "All right," he said, exhaling heavily. "Thanks."

The chief rose, placing a hand on Danny's shoulder. "What if she be right?"

"She's not," Danny said flatly. "I've hoped over

and over again that some child would turn out to be my Noah. And it never was."

He felt, more than saw, the cop shrug. "Okay. What you gonna do? I can take her back to Kauai since you canceled Dr. Atada's visit."

Danny shook his head instantly. Then he wondered just what in the hell he was doing. He should get her out of his life. But…he was curious about her kid. Even if it wasn't Noah, it was still a compelling story.

He saw the two professionals onto their launch back to Kauai, then sped back up the path to the house. "Where is she?" he asked Leilani.

"She sittin' outside by the pool," she replied. "You want lemonade?"

"That would be nice." Danny turned and walked out to the pool deck. Sydney sat in a lounge near the shallow end, big sunglasses on her nose and a slim black tank suit covering her curves. It wasn't a revealing suit by any means, but she still was so attractive he caught his breath. *Knock it off,* he told himself. The last thing he needed was to get involved with her.

"Hello," she said as he approached. "Have you watched the video?"

"I was watching live," he said tersely.

"Oh. Good." She paused, then leaned forward anxiously. "Do you have any questions I can answer?"

He shrugged. "Not really. You covered everything I wanted to know."

She nodded and relaxed. "I can't believe I forgot all that," she said ruefully. "I wonder if I was afraid to remember it. I knew before I came here that if I did get the chance to meet with you, it would be a pretty explosive topic."

"What would you have done if things had turned out differently, if you hadn't gotten to talk to me?"

"Gone home and approached you through your family or through a lawyer, I imagine. I hadn't even considered that you might refuse to see me. I thought you'd be thrilled at the possibility of finding your son." She sounded as if she couldn't comprehend his attitude.

He sighed. "Sydney…" Suddenly he realized that he didn't think she was lying anymore. She wasn't a gold digger and he was ashamed that he'd leaped to the wrong conclusion so quickly. He lowered himself to the end of the chaise on which she sat, and she obligingly moved her feet and legs to one side. "I'm sorry. For not believing you. For getting angry. I know you're not the kind of person who would use a child as a bargaining chip or a blackmail item."

"It's all right," she said. "I can't imagine how you must feel. I think I'd die if someone took Nick."

"You'd want to," he said soberly.

She flushed a deep scarlet. "I'm so sorry. I didn't mean— I didn't intend to remind you—" She stopped, distress radiating from her as she realized what she'd said.

"It's okay." He took pity on her. "It's not that I wouldn't love to find Noah. But I've been through this so many times. In the first couple of years occasionally there was a legitimate lead. They always went nowhere. There were also at least twice that many fake leads, with people claiming they would return my son for a price."

Sydney was silent for a moment. Just as he was about to ask her what she was thinking, she whispered, "Do you still miss him so much? Still think about him every day?"

Danny nodded. "Both of them. Every day."

She sucked in a sharp breath. "How do you bear it?"

"I don't have a choice," he said simply. Then, too raw to continue in that vein, he said, "So tell me, did you ever think about placing the baby for adoption once you realized the mother wasn't coming back?"

Sydney's face relaxed, and a small smile played around the edges of her mouth. "No. Never. Nick had me wrapped around his little finger from the first day I held him." Her voice thickened and he saw her swallow. "I guess I'd always imagined I'd be a mother someday. But 'someday' was in the future, just a hazy dream. And of course, I'd be married." She smiled. "But I never anticipated the joy that motherhood brought. Taking on a baby was the last thing on my agenda, but sometimes I feel as if it were fate. He…needed me, and I guess I needed him, too."

Danny sat silently. Joy. Yes, it was an apt description of the giddy happiness he'd known in that one short year he'd been granted with his own child.

"It's devastating," she said, her gaze fixed on the ripples bouncing across the pool, "to think that I've enjoyed Nick's life while his own mother couldn't bear to live without him, while his own father has been deprived of him. I know I shouldn't feel guilty, because I didn't know. But somehow I do."

God, there she went again. He didn't know what to say to her utter certainty that she had his son.

"What are you thinking?" she asked.

He raised his hands helplessly, clearing his throat and hoping like hell he didn't completely break down in front of her. "In my heart—" he touched his chest "—I've accepted that my son is dead. God, I just don't think I can bear to have my hopes raised and dashed again." The last words were as anguished as the pain tearing at him.

Sydney made a small sound and slid forward. Her arms went around him in a physical expression of comfort much like that he imagined she used to comfort her son after one of his nightmares.

He dropped his head to her shoulder and simply breathed in the sweet, feminine fragrance that was Sydney. His arms came up around her slender back and pulled her closer, and he felt her press a kiss to his temple just above the level of his ear.

For the longest time, he held her, liking the way her arms held him to her, the way her soft curves felt against him, the balm that her understanding and acceptance brought.

"I wish," she said after a while, "that we hadn't met under these circumstances."

Danny lifted his head and the moment changed.

Sexual awareness suddenly charged the air around them as he gazed into her blue eyes. "So do I," he said in a low, rough tone as he set his mouth on hers.

# *Seven*

If he'd stopped to think about it, Danny never would have kissed her. But once he had her mouth beneath his again, her slim body wrapped in his arms, there was no way he could stop.

Just as before, she responded to him without hesitation. Her arms twined about his shoulders, and one small hand slid up into his hair, gently rubbing over his scalp. He shuddered. It had been so long since he'd made love to a woman that his body instantly wanted to finish what he'd started.

He bent her backward with the force of his kiss, but she never moved away, only clung more tightly.

"Sydney, I have— Oh!" Leilani's voice startled

him. He felt Sydney jolt in his arms, and immediately she began to struggle.

"Sorry," Leilani said, already backing away. "This can wait until tomorrow."

As her footsteps receded hurriedly across the stone tiles of the terrace floor, Danny gently made sure Sydney was upright before he released her. For a moment, he just sat with his hands hanging between his knees. How the hell did this happen? He'd never had trouble keeping his hands off a woman before, but it seemed as if he could barely be in the same room with Sydney without giving in to the need to touch her, hold her, kiss her. He'd better get out of here while he still could make himself move.

"Danny?" Sydney hesitated.

"Yeah?" His voice was little more than a growl, and he cleared his throat. Man, she was potent.

"I'm attracted to you," she informed him.

He couldn't prevent a burst of startled laughter. "No kidding. And it's sure no secret that I'm attracted to you."

She blushed and he chuckled. As the sound hit the air, he was briefly amazed. He'd laughed more since Sydney had arrived than he had in years.

When he straightened and stood, she stood as well. "This is a problem," she said. "I'm very attracted to you. But it has to be separate from the other stuff that we have to deal with."

He sobered instantly. "I know."

She sighed. "I've never felt like this before."

"Attracted?" He attempted humor, but the heaviness of the subject before them squashed it flat.

She gave him a bittersweet smile. "It isn't just physical." She lifted her hand and briefly tapped a finger over her heart. "I'm starting to care for you."

He didn't know what to say. *"I'm starting to care for you, too"* absolutely wasn't acceptable. He couldn't get involved with her. With anyone.

Sydney pushed out of his arms and swung her legs off the chaise. Her movements were stiff and jerky and he realized he'd waited too long to speak. "Sydney—"

But she cut him off with a raised palm. "Don't. It's my problem, not yours. I'll be leaving soon and you can go back to your quiet routine with no interruptions." Somehow, she made it sound incredibly unappealing.

As she walked away, a surprising sense of loss swept over him. And a realization that he should have acknowledged before. When he'd decided to take her on the helicopter tour earlier, he'd been looking forward to seeing her face as they toured the islands from the air, looking forward to something for the first time he could remember since he lost his family.

It probably was a good thing she was leaving soon. Sydney was beautiful, intelligent, tenderhearted and compassionate; she had a gentle sense of humor and the ability to put anyone at ease. She was the kind of woman he would want to get to know better—if he ever were to look for another woman again.

But he wasn't, he reminded himself. He'd had all the heartbreak he wanted to taste in one lifetime. No way was he going to get involved with someone again.

Later in the afternoon, Danny walked into the kitchen and saw Sydney on the phone.

"Under no circumstances can he bring back a puppy, Mom," she was saying. "I work all day. I can't take care of a dog."

She listened for a moment and then laughed. "Okay. I love you, too. Give Nick a big hug from Mommy and tell him I'll be home soon."

Danny had gotten a glass of ice water and quietly began to leave the kitchen, trying not to appear to be eavesdropping. But as she hung up the phone, she said, "You don't have to leave, Danny. I'm done."

He paused in the doorway. Her tone was natural and friendly, as if they'd never kissed, never discussed the serious things they had. "Trouble at home?" he asked, trying to match her casual tone.

She smiled. "No. But my son has my parents wrapped around his little finger and he figures if he can talk them into getting him a puppy before I get back, he'll be able to keep it." The smile slipped. "I'd love to be able to let him have a dog. But it simply isn't practical right now."

"Because you work?"

"Not only that. We live in an apartment. No yard. No pets allowed, anyway. I've been thinking of buying a house when my lease is up, but frankly, I'm a little intimidated by the thought of owning a home and being responsible for all the maintenance. I've considered a condo, but even that isn't exceptionally workable for anything but a fairly small dog. Nick, of course, has visions of Irish wolfhounds and Newfoundlands."

Danny chuckled. "Does your son understand why he can't get a dog?" It was a clumsy redirection but ever since he'd heard her on the phone he'd been consumed by curiosity. Right there, at the other end of that line, was a child she believed to be his son. That wasn't true, but he couldn't help wondering what the little boy was like, anyway.

Sydney didn't appear to think the question intrusive. "I think so," she said, "but he doesn't want to understand." She smiled fondly. "Little manipulator."

He didn't need to hear anything more about her son, Danny told himself. But the urge to stay in her company was too strong to resist. "I'm going to walk down to the beach," he told her. "You're welcome to come along."

She hesitated. "Thank you," she finally said. "I changed my original flight plans today. I'll be leaving tomorrow. One more walk on the beach would be lovely."

She was leaving tomorrow. He should be relieved. Glad to regain his solitude. But all he could think was that he was never going to see her again.

She ran to her room for her beach shoes, and Danny went outside to wait at the top of the steps leading down the cliff. He thought of the day he'd first seen Sydney lying on the rocks below him. His life had been quiet, orderly, predictable just a few short days ago. Now he felt like one big mass of conflicted emotion.

"Sorry I took so long."

He turned as Sydney called to him. She was carrying a wide-brimmed hat and her light sundress rippled around her slender body as she came toward him.

She looked beautiful and happy in the sunlight pouring over them, and Danny felt his heart squeeze painfully. He'd never felt like this before, either. It was difficult to admit, but it was true.

Felicia. For the first time in a long time he allowed himself to think of his wife. He couldn't remember her face anymore, except for frozen shots from photographs they'd taken.

"A penny for your thoughts." Sydney had come to a halt in front of him. Her hair blew across her face in the light breeze and without thinking, he put up a hand and smoothed it away, tucking it behind one ear. Sydney went still for a moment. Then, in a movement so subtle he wouldn't have recognized it if he wasn't so tuned in to her, she took a step away, ostensibly to look out over the ocean, withdrawing from him.

He forced himself not to reach for her. Instead, he snorted. "My thoughts aren't worth a penny."

That got her attention. "Yes," she said quietly, firmly. "They are."

He shrugged. "I was thinking about my wife, if you

really want to know." He indicated the path down to the beach. "Shall we?"

Sydney let him take the lead, showing her where to step until they reached the stairs near the steepest section. "What was her name?" she asked, as if their conversation had never stopped.

"Felicia."

"How pretty."

He nodded, his gaze on the steps below them. "She matched her name. Blue eyes and blond hair. Very pretty."

"How did you meet?"

He turned and looked up at her. "In rehab."

If he'd thought to shock her, he was disappointed. "What kind of rehab?"

"Drug and alcohol. It was actually a treatment center for suicidal people."

"You tried to kill yourself? How old were you?"

"Twenty-one."

"A vulnerable age. More so if you've suffered the kind of trauma you did as a child."

The sun was so bright it was making his eyes water. He couldn't be getting teary just because she offered unconditional acceptance.

"I swallowed every pill I could find in my mother's medicine cabinet." He gave a humorless smile. "And believe me, there were plenty."

"Did you change your mind once you'd taken them?"

Danny shook his head. "No." He hated to admit it,

but it was true. "I really thought the world would be better without me. But my mother's housekeeper came in on her day off and found me."

Sydney made a small sound and her hand touched his back briefly. "I'm glad she did."

"Trent and my father convinced me to give in-patient treatment a try when I was released from the hospital afterward." It had been the lowest of many low points in his life at the time. And why was he telling Sydney all this? She'd asked about Felicia, not a chronicle of The Misfortunes of Danny Crosby.

"Anyway," he said, "we met there. She also had tried suicide. I guess we helped each other recover."

"And fell in love," she said softly. "Only she couldn't be as strong as you when Noah was taken away."

He nodded, not looking back at her. But he couldn't help comparing what he'd felt for Felicia with the feelings ruffling his composure now. They'd grown together naturally as a result of their mutual experiences and recovery. He couldn't ever recall feeling the wild, undeniable attraction that he fought every second he spent in Sydney's company.

But he'd loved Felicia. Surely he had.

At the bottom of the steps, they walked across the warm sand to the water's edge.

"It's so beautiful," Sydney said as she looked seaward.

Danny followed her gaze. It was indeed beautiful, but to him, the spumes of white water shooting into the air where the ocean met the reef at the outer edges of the small lagoon looked deadly as well. "It's deceptive," he said. "Look out there."

Sydney obediently looked in the direction he pointed. "That tiny opening is the only break in the reef all along this little bay. Any boat that comes ashore has to come through there."

"Apparently, I missed it," she said lightly, but he could hear remembered fear in her voice.

"Fortunately, you made it past the reef somehow."

"Thank heaven," she said.

"Have you told your family about your accident?"

She shook her head. "No. It would just have worried my parents. And Nick already has enough anxiety issues with the nightmares without me adding to it."

"Tell me more about him." Danny winced at the eager look she sent him. "Not," he cautioned, "because I think he's my son. Just because."

A little of the light faded from her face, but she nodded, turning and beginning to walk along the beach. "He's tall for his age," she said, "but skinny as a rail. He's got big blue eyes and this fine, flyaway blond hair that gets tangled really easily if I don't keep it pretty short."

As he fell into step beside her, an instant image of Felicia's corn-silk tresses shot into Danny's mind. Coincidence.

"He likes to play computer games," she went on. "He hasn't even started school yet but he already can read. I signed him up for peewee soccer, and he loves it. His best friend is the coach's son and when they're together we've learned not to take our eyes off them for a minute. If Nick and Zachary are quiet, it usually means they're in trouble," she said, chuckling. "Let's see, what else? We go swimming every Saturday evening at the local Y. He's a total fish in the water and he even jumps off the diving board."

Danny found that he couldn't help smiling at the image.

"He loves stories. I read to him every night before bed. It's probably my favorite time of day, after his bath and his snack, when he's winding down for the night."

Her love for her son was evident in every word, every expression that crossed her mobile features. It was only natural, he supposed, to compare the little boy's life to his own, Sydney to his mother.

Had anyone ever loved him like that? There was no question in his mind that Sydney's son knew he was loved, knew he was the center of her universe. There also was no question that his own mother hadn't even considered that any of her children might need nurturing of any kind. She hadn't been capable of it.

*Then she'd had no business ever having children.* He'd lost any feeling he'd had for his mother years ago. It was sad, but as one of his counselors had noted, necessary for his survival. And actually, because he'd never known what having a real relationship with a loving parent was, he hadn't missed it—until now, when the emotion bubbling in Sydney's voice showed him clearly what she felt for her son. "You love him very much," he said aloud.

She smiled. "Yes. He's the greatest kid in the world."

He tried to imagine his own mother saying something like that. Didn't happen. Never would. Sheila Crosby was as unlike Sydney Aston as the light sand was from the black cliffs just down the beach.

He glanced at his companion. She had her hair bundled up beneath the straw hat, exposing her long, elegant neck and the delicate bones of her shoulders. A light breeze had plastered her dress against her body, outlining the thrust of breasts, the soft roundness of hips and a long, slender length of thigh. He'd felt that body against him, knew the pleasure that merely touching her gave him. Out of nowhere, a rush of need surged through him, and he almost reached for her before he quelled the urge.

He stopped walking. Sydney didn't notice right away and he stood on the wide, flat beach watching her sashay along ahead of him. She was totally unaware of what she did to him. Well, maybe not totally, but darn near. He'd bet she had no clue as to how desperately he yearned to take back to the house, to a quiet room with a soft bed and even softer sheets. He'd strip that fluttery dress off and lay her down—

"Danny?"

She had turned and was watching him quizzically. He hoped she would keep her eyes on his face or she would know what direction his thoughts had gone. Quickly, he lengthened his stride and caught up with her. *Forget it,* he told himself. The last thing he needed was to get any more involved with Sydney Aston, either physically or emotionally. Caring led inevitably to pain, sooner or later. But the reminder sounded hollow and cowardly.

"Sorry," he said. "Guess I was daydreaming. Tell me more about Nick."

She shrugged. "I think I mentioned just about everything he's involved in— Oh, wait, I almost forgot. He belongs to a boy's club at our church. Several of the little boys from his Sunday-school class are in it. They meet for an hour on Tuesday evenings and have a blast." She grimaced. "It gets interesting sometimes when he needs help with a project."

"Such as?"

"Such as the go-cart derby. Or a recent one involving making a simple rocket ship." She shook her head, laughing. "My mechanical and technical skills are sadly lacking, so he's at a real disadvantage compared to some of the other little boys whose fathers have woodworking setups in their garages."

"Isn't there anyone close who could help?"

She nodded. "My dad occasionally comes down if there's something big he can help Nick put together. And the guy next door is a mechanic. He volunteered to help out if we ever need him."

He wondered if the guy next door was married. "What else do they do? Do they go camping like Scouts do?"

"They do. And they work on service projects around the community. In April, we picked up litter at a local park. Last month, we held an ice-cream social for the residents of a nursing home. The boys even helped churn the ice cream." She shook her head, still smiling. "That was a tough one for Nick since he can't eat ice cream."

"Because of his lactose intolerance."

"Right. Dairy products give him terrible stomach pains."

Danny felt a chill ripple down his spine, totally unexpected in the tropical air. He'd almost forgotten what she'd said about that—probably on purpose. He almost missed a step, but focused on continuing to put one foot in front of the other, to walk along the beach as if what she'd just said had no import.

"He drinks soy milk," she went on, "and usually doesn't seem to miss the whole dairy thing. It's a small price to pay for feeling good, especially after the other things he's been through."

"Other things?" His voice sounded very cool and calm, as if some other person were speaking. But when he looked down, his hands were shaking, and he balled them into loose fists before she could comment.

She nodded in response to his question. "I noticed very early on that he sometimes looked a little…gray after any kind of exertion. Twice right after Margo left, he got so short of breath I almost called an ambulance. When I finally realized she wasn't coming back, I took him to a pediatrician one of my co-workers recommended. He had a complete physical. And that's when I found out Nick had a heart defect."

*A heart defect.* "What kind?" His voice was so hoarse he had to clear his throat and repeat the words. Congenital heart defects ran in his family. His father had lived with one undetected most of his life, but had had a brother who had died young. And Jackson Reiss, Danny's recently discovered half brother, had a son who'd been diagnosed with the same disorder.

Sydney glanced at him. "Are you all right?"

He nodded, not even trying to speak again.

"It's a congenital malformation," she said, "that's usually inherited. Often there are no visible symptoms. Apparently healthy young adult men just keel over, like that ice skater did ten years ago. But Nick had an additional complication that caused him to have trouble even as an infant. It's another reason I don't think he was Margo's biological child. I can't believe she wouldn't have noticed and had it corrected if he really were hers. The doctor said he really should have had surgery months ago and that he was lucky to have survived this long. Danny?"

"Noah had a heart problem," he said. "I'm sure— was sure—he couldn't have lived very long without surgery." God, was it possible? What Sydney had just described sounded extremely similar to his family's genetic heart ailment.

Sydney put a hand to her heart, and he could see a rapid pulse fluttering beneath the fragile skin of her throat. "So Nick really could be Noah." Her face had lost whatever color it had had. "I thought he might be," she said, and her voice was quavery, "and I thought I was prepared, but…" Tears welled in her eyes. Then she took a deep breath and seemed to dredge a hidden core of steel from beneath her soft exterior. "We need to have a DNA test done," she said. "We probably could compare the medical records and his blood type, but I'd rather just do the DNA test. And then we'd never have any doubts."

A DNA test. His heart was pounding so hard it felt as if it were going to leap right out of his chest and take off down the beach. He couldn't breathe. This child— her child—wasn't his. Was he? He couldn't be.

Could he?

"Sit down," Sydney said, tugging on his arm.

They both sat side by side on the warm sand, look-ing out over the ocean. But Danny wasn't seeing ocean. In his mind's eye, a chubby baby staggered to-ward him, a baby who'd just begun to walk alone. Two tiny, pearly white teeth on both top and bottom gleamed as he grinned.

He dropped his head onto the arms he'd crossed over his drawn-up knees, feeling unmanly tears sting-ing his eyes. At his side, Sydney placed a palm in the middle of his back and rubbed a small, soothing cir-cle over and over again.

He pressed his forehead hard against his arms. God, he wanted so badly to believe it was possible. But what if he got his hopes up and then learned Nick Aston wasn't his? It wasn't like it hadn't happened before, he reminded himself. And he couldn't go through it again.

Aloud, he said, "It's got to be a coincidence. Just like the lactose thing."

He'd forgotten he hadn't said anything about that, but Sydney was quick. "Noah was lactose intolerant, too?"

He swallowed and nodded without lifting his head.

"Danny, we have to have a test done." Her voice was insistent. "Don't you want to know?"

He shrugged. "I already know."

But did he? What if— No. Noah *wasn't* alive and well and in Sydney's capable hands. Of all the fates that he'd agonized over his son suffering, living in happy comfort hadn't been one of them.

But he was going to have to have this testing done, if only to convince Sydney that he wasn't the father of her child. "All right," he finally said. He lifted his head and met her gaze, and saw that she had tears running down her cheeks. The lump he'd swallowed rose again and he had to take a deep breath before he could speak further. "I'll have the testing done. Let me make some calls. We can probably get them done without much of a wait."

It would make Sydney feel better, he told himself. She honestly believed she had his son. He'd humor her until he could prove that she was wrong, as he knew she must be.

But the tiny flame of hope that had been lit inside him was impossible to extinguish.

# *Eight*

He didn't invite her to dine with him that evening.

When Sydney walked into the kitchen, Leilani pointed to a small patio just beyond the breakfast nook, one she'd never used before. "I feed you there tonight."

"Thank you." She tried not to mind. She wasn't an invited guest and she knew she'd intruded into the quiet, predictable world Danny had built for himself. And she'd gotten what she came for, in any case, during those emotional moments on the beach earlier. He might say he didn't believe her but now at least he was willing to concede it was a possibility.

She felt tears well again in her eyes at the mere thought of the devastation she'd witnessed on Danny's face. Dear God, how did anyone live through the death of a child? And in his case, it was even worse because his son had simply vanished. Torn from the fabric of their lives without any warning. She thought of what Danny had told her about his troubled life. She'd never felt the least bit suicidal but she wasn't sure how she'd feel if something happened to Nick. She couldn't assign blame to Felicia Crosby for not wanting to live, she told herself firmly.

Still, she knew deep in her heart that she could never do that to those who loved her. Especially if she had a loving husband who was grieving as well. Hadn't Felicia known how badly Danny needed her?

She sighed. Perhaps she simply hadn't been able to deal with anything but her own pain.

Dinner was as lovely as always, and the little terrace had its own striking view of the sea. But her aching heart interfered with her enjoyment of her last night in Hawaii, and as soon as she'd finished eating, she returned to her room to get her things organized again for her departure from the island. Her flight left early in the morning and Johnny would be taking her to the airport shortly after sunrise.

It was too quiet in the big house. She was still troubled by the events of the afternoon. Danny had looked so shaken. So sad. She hated that she was the one who'd made him feel that way again. Who'd made him think of what he'd lost.

Still, he was going to get it back. Why couldn't he see that? After what he'd told her, there was no doubt anymore in her mind that she was the mother of Noah Crosby.

She couldn't bear thinking about it all anymore, and she snapped on the television, hunting for something to occupy her mind. Music videos. She stopped at that channel, letting the music wash over her. They were doing a special on songs with romantic themes, many of which had soft, dreamy melodies and close harmonies, and as she folded the clothing she needed to return to Leilani, she sang softly.

Someone rapped on her open bedroom door.

Sydney stifled a startled cry as she whirled. Danny stood framed in the doorway, a crooked smile quirking his lips.

"Sorry," he said. "Didn't mean to scare you."

"It's all right." She let out her breath on a sigh.

"I, uh, came to tell you that I've arranged the testing."

Her eyes widened. "That was fast."

He nodded. "How does the day after tomorrow sound to you? I made a reservation for myself on your flight back to Portland and we can have the testing done at a lab there."

"Oh, my." She dropped the muumuu she was folding. The day after tomorrow…? And if the results were what she expected, what she was certain they would be, what then? Would she just hand her son over to his birth father and walk away? Everything in her rejected the idea, but the bottom line was that she had no claim to Danny's son. Other than the fact that she'd been his adoptive mother for nearly four years and she loved him desperately. The thought was so devastating she couldn't process it.

"All right." Her voice wavered. "I have a sample of Nick's hair you can take with you."

"Hey." He crossed the room in three long strides and picked up the muumuu before she could even command her body to retrieve it. When she made no move to take it, he let it drop into a colorful puddle on the bed. "This is what you wanted, remember?" His voice was gentle. She noticed he didn't say it was what he wanted, just as he'd carefully avoided voicing any hope that Nick might be his son.

She nodded, unable to speak for the lump that clogged her throat again.

Silence fell between them. The muted music from the television played softly and she felt the tears she'd been trying to hold back escape and begin rolling down her cheeks.

"Aw, Sydney, don't." Danny took a step closer and then she felt his hands on her body, urging her into his arms. He pulled her close, drawing her into his lap as he settled on the edge of her bed.

She closed her eyes and clasped her arms around his neck, turning her head into his neck as he began to rock her. Slowly, they swayed back and forth, barely moving, his body brushing tantalizingly against hers. It was a moving embrace and she responded to it, letting herself relax and savor the moment.

Danny drew her even closer to him. One hand slid

more firmly around her back, holding her against him so that she became vividly aware of his hard thighs beneath her bottom. The other hand slid down her back and around to her hip, shaping and smoothing the curve he found there. He felt good against her, strong and firm and all male, and she pressed herself against him without thought, feeling only how right it was. How right they were together.

"Sydney." Danny bent his head and whispered her name against her ear. The moist heat of his breath brushing over the sensitive shell made her shiver, a sheerly sexual thrill running through her. She knew what he wanted and because she wanted it, too, she raised her head.

He kissed her the moment her face turned up to his, sliding his lips onto hers so gently that one moment they weren't kissing, the next they were. He shaped her mouth with care, his tongue doing a stealthy, sensual dance around and over the closed line of her lips until she allowed him a deeper foray and followed his lead. The moment changed, lazy and gentle giving way to more demanding passion, arms shifting and clutching, mouths seeking, bodies straining.

Suddenly Danny tore his mouth from hers. "Wait," he gasped. "We are not doing this." He sounded as if he was trying to convince himself. "You're leaving tomorrow."

Yes. She had to. She'd never wanted so badly to ignore her responsibilities and simply live in the moment. But she couldn't.

There was a tense silence.

She rose and walked around the bed to pick up the clothing she'd been folding when he walked in. She drew a deep breath. "I am," she said.

Danny looked at the floor. Every line of his big body was tense and she could almost feel the desire ricocheting around the room. His pants molded to his strong thighs and she swallowed, seeing the evidence of his need for her that he couldn't hide. She should be thanking him for stopping, but it was all she could do not to rush across the room and plaster herself to him, fit herself against him, shed her clothes and beg him to take her.

She gritted her teeth and stood rooted to the floor, squeezing her eyes tightly shut. After a moment, she heard his footsteps retreating and the door gently clicking shut.

She knew an instant sense of loss when she opened her eyes the next morning. Early-morning light was flooding the room and she suddenly remembered that today was the day she was leaving. Misery threatened to sweep her feet right out from beneath her, but she stiffened her resolve and rose. Some things just weren't meant to be. Danny was never going to let himself feel, love, live again. She had to accept that.

With necessary haste, she showered, dressed and finished packing her things.

Finally, there was nothing left to do but go.

Danny stood at the foot of the stairs as she descended. "Ready?" he asked.

She nodded, smiling at him as impersonally as she could, trying desperately to be friendly but not familiar. "Johnny already got my bags."

Danny nodded. But he didn't quite meet her eyes as he stepped back to allow her to precede him out the door. Then, just as she was about to slide onto the ATV for the ride down to the dock, he touched her arm. Barely touched her arm, she noticed, and then withdrew his fingers as if she'd burned him.

"It's not you," he said quietly. "I hope you know that. But I stopped feeling a long time ago." He made a short, choppy gesture. "And I don't want to change."

She positioned herself on the vehicle and looked straight ahead. "I haven't asked you to change." *I will not cry. I will not cry. I will not cry.*

Danny hesitated for a moment, but when she didn't speak or look at him, he climbed on in front of her. As he kicked the ATV into gear, she was forced to put her arms around him to hang on. The urge to give in to the tears was strong, and she had to fight not to simply lay her cheek against his back and sob.

But he'd made it more than clear that he wasn't interested, that his apparent interest would have been nothing more than simple sex to him. Oh, she was probably wrong about that. It wasn't simple at all. Danny had been dealt more heartbreak in one lifetime that any person deserved, and she knew why he didn't want to be interested, even if there had been sparks between them.

Sparks? More like fifty-foot-high flames.

Nevertheless, if he wanted to pretend theirs was no more than a casual attraction, easily forgotten, there was nothing she could do to change his mind.

Making love with Danny would have been far more than casual to her. She resolutely refused to think about exactly what it could have been. It didn't matter anymore.

Sydney sat beside him on the flight back to the mainland. But she might as well have been at the other end of the plane, Danny decided. She responded when he spoke to her, but otherwise, she appeared to be totally unaware of his presence. The special connection they'd shared on the island might never have been.

It was just as well, he reminded himself. He didn't need, didn't want any emotional entanglements. He would go to Portland with Sydney, have this DNA test and show her that her child couldn't possibly be his son. Then he'd come back to his quiet island, where one day flowed into another with barely a ripple and nothing disturbed the peace he'd found there.

Then he thought of the way Sydney had looked in the lamplight last night, her eyes deep pools of heat. He thought of the silky feel of her skin, the fresh scent of her hair, the soft little sounds she made deep in her throat when he touched her. He thought of the way her understanding presence soothed the raw spots that still oozed inside him. His chest felt tight and he put up an uncertain hand to massage the area right over his heart.

He had a feeling his island wasn't going to be the same without Sydney.

"I'm sorry." God, had he just said that aloud?

Sydney turned to him, eyebrows raised in polite inquiry. Her tone was distant and cool. "I beg your pardon?"

He took a deep breath. He had to try to make her understand. The last thing he wanted was for her to believe she'd been just a…convenience for him. "I'm sorry," he said again. "I should never have come to your room last night."

"Let's forget about it," she said, turning her face away from him.

"I can't," he said baldly. "I don't want to hurt you, Sydney. And I'm afraid that's exactly what I'm doing."

She didn't answer, didn't even tilt her head to indicate that she'd heard him.

"I can't be with you," he said, somewhat desperate to make her see. "It's not you. It's me. I just…there's nothing left in me to give you. Any woman. And if you keep believing there's more, you're only going to get hurt." More quietly, he reiterated, "And that's the last thing I want."

"I heard you the first time." Her voice was so completely flat and devoid of expression that he knew it already was too late. He'd already hurt her more than she deserved.

A sense of futility and frustration enveloped him. Damn it. He should have sent her back the very day he'd found her, instead of giving in to his curiosity—and all right, his instant attraction to her. He'd known from the beginning he couldn't get into any more relationships.

* * *

As the flight stopped at the gate and passengers began to disembark, Danny stood and handed down the single small carryon she'd brought. Then he stepped back and waited for her to precede him from the plane.

She was all too aware of his tall form right behind her as they headed up the ramp and into Concourse D of Portland International. As they passed the gate security and moved out into the public part of the airport, other passengers rushed into the waiting arms of families. One woman knelt and tearfully embraced a small boy of about Nick's size, and the sight reminded her of something. "Would you like to come along to my parents' place? You could meet Nick, get to know him and see a little bit of his life—"

But Danny was already shaking his head. "No thanks. I have business to take care of while I'm here. I'll be in touch after the test results come back."

She nodded, not trusting herself to speak. His blue eyes were remote, his thoughts shielded from her, and she wondered if she'd ever felt more alone. Straightening her shoulders, she said, "All right. See you then." And picking up her bag, she hurried off down the terminal toward baggage claim.

After a moment, Danny caught up with her. She saw him from her peripheral vision, pacing along beside her, though he didn't say anything more. Abruptly, her throat closed up and she knew she couldn't just stand there with him until the bags arrived. Thankfully, she noted a ladies' room sign just ahead, and as they passed it, she veered off and entered the women's sanctum. There was a long bench and a couple of chairs usually reserved for nursing mothers in a room adjacent to the bathroom itself, though the place was deserted at the moment. She sank down into one of the chairs, letting her carryon thud to the floor at her feet. Then she pressed the heels of her hands to her eyes and willed the tears away.

After a few moments and several deep breaths, she finally felt she had regained a bit of her nearly vanished composure. She glanced at her watch. It would take at least ten minutes for her rolling suitcase to be unloaded and brought into the terminal. She wasn't leaving this restroom for a little while.

She hauled out a box of raisins she'd put in her purse as an antidote for airplane food. She hadn't been able to eat on the flight and she still wasn't hungry, but she forced herself to eat them. Her head ached so she took some painkillers with water from the bottle in her carryon. Then she washed her face and hands and dug through her purse until she found her makeup. She might not feel top-grade, but the slight color she'd acquired made her skin glow and intensified the blue of her eyes, making her look fresh and healthy. That was good. Her mother was already worried enough.

Finally, she stood and hefted her bag. By now the luggage should have arrived. She took her time descending to the baggage claim area and purposely didn't look around at other people as she found the flashing sign that proclaimed her flight's number. A crowd had gathered around the conveyor belt and she walked down close to the point at which the luggage emerged from the flap on the wall. Lady Luck must have taken pity on her because she was barely in place when her suitcase came barreling down the ramp onto the belt.

Sydney heaved it off into an upright position, pulled up the handle and stacked her carryon atop it. Then she tilted the bag onto its wheeled side and began to maneuver through the crowd of jostling strangers. It wasn't far to the curb outside under the huge glassed-in canopy. That was where she would meet the shuttle bus that would take her out to the long-term parking lot where she'd left her car.

A tall man stepped into her path and she swerved to avoid him, realizing as she did so who it was, and her heart sank. She'd been hoping to get away without having to see him again.

"Hey," Danny said. "Let me get that for you." He already had his own large duffel over one shoulder and he reached for her suitcase as he spoke.

"No thanks." She deftly rolled the luggage back out of his reach. "I've got it." She sent an impersonal smile in the general direction of his face. "I guess we'll talk in a couple of days." And without giving him a chance for one more word, she wheeled her suitcase around him and headed through the automatic doors to the shuttle line.

She fought tears several times on the drive to her

apartment, but once she was home again, standing amid all the things she'd forgotten just a few days ago—had it really only been a few days since she'd met Danny?—she forced the hurt into hiding. *This* was her life. Not the idyllic experience she'd just had on a tropical island with the most charismatic, attractive man she'd ever met in her life.

"Hello, Everett." Nancy Allen stood in the open door of Everett Baker's small apartment. Her eyes were warm and looked suspiciously moist, and before he could gather his wits, she stepped forward and wrapped her arms around his neck, pressing her soft, wonderfully familiar body tightly to his. "Oh," she said in a voice that made him pretty sure she was trying hard not to cry, "I'm so glad you made bail."

"How did you find out?" He couldn't resist putting his own arms around her, burying his face in her fragrant hair and adjusting the fit of their bodies until he'd found that particular sweet, perfectly aligned plane that always took his breath away.

"I was sitting in the back of the courtroom," she said. "I saw your father make the offer."

"My real father. Terrence Logan." He pulled back far enough to see her face.

Nancy nodded. Her gaze searched his face. "How do you feel about what's happened?"

He hesitated. "You mean finding out who I really am…was?"

She nodded.

He shook his head, letting his bewilderment show. "I don't know. Terrible." Then the certainty that he'd lived with since he'd been arrested returned full force. "Nancy, you didn't need to come here. I mean, I understand how you must feel—"

"Worried to death? Sad and heartsick for you?" She took his face between her hands. "Oh, Everett, I wish I'd known. Maybe I could have done something."

"You did," he told her soberly. "Because of you, I found the courage to stand up to Charlie Prescott and go to the cops. After you and I…became friends, I realized that whatever Charlie wanted from me, friendship was pretty far down on the list."

"Became friends," Nancy repeated. "Is that how you think of us?" Her eyes were still soft and so very warm, and she hadn't stepped away from him. Yet.

"No," he said. He would be honest from now on, no matter what it cost him. "I think of you as the most wonderful thing ever to happen in my life. But, Nancy, the things I did were terrible. I wouldn't blame you if you never wanted to talk to me again."

Nancy slowly withdrew her arms and he let her step away from him. But to his surprise, she didn't leave. Instead, she took his hand and led him toward the battered couch in his cramped living room.

Nancy put a hand over his. Tears sparkled in her eyes. "Oh, Everett, I only wish you'd told me. We could have gone to the authorities together."

"I know." He turned his palm up and felt as if he'd been granted a miracle when Nancy laced her fingers through his. "I'm sorry." Shame coursed through him yet again.

"Don't be," she said fiercely. "Anyone who lived through a childhood experience like yours can be forgiven for making mistakes. Charlie Prescott chose you because he thought you were vulnerable."

"He was right." And he despised himself for being so weak.

"Do you remember your own family?" she asked. It was the first time she'd sounded hesitant, and he realized she didn't want to pry.

"A little." He studied their clasped hands. "More things are coming back to me every day."

"Someday," she said, "I'd like to hear as much as you want to share with me about your childhood."

He sighed. "There's a lot you probably don't want to hear. The couple who took me, the Bakers, weren't exactly role models for the American family."

"Were you abused?" Her voice was very soft.

He nodded. "I got beaten a lot. But even worse was the stuff they used to say to me."

"You know," she said, "I've seen a lot of abused children in my line of work. And it's so sad to see how many of them will cling to an abusive parent even after they've been horribly damaged. Apparently, a bad parent seems better than no sense of security, of belonging, at all. I imagine Charlie realized you needed someone, or something, to validate you."

He nodded. "He was right. I believed I was stupid and worthless. I guess if you get told that often enough you start to believe it."

Nancy nodded. "You internalized it. But you know he was wrong, don't you?"

He attempted a crooked smile. "Let's just say I'm working on my self-image."

Nancy frowned, and when she spoke, her voice was uncharacteristically sharp. "It's not a question of smart or stupid, it's one of how your environment shaped your need for relationships. You're a very smart man, Everett, and a very strong one." She hesitated, then said, "There are doctors and counselors who specialize in deprogramming people who have been brainwashed, which is essentially what was done to you. If I could find one to help you deal with your past, would you see that person?"

He couldn't believe she still would bother with him after everything he'd told her. And yet, she hadn't run, hadn't gotten angry or disgusted. She'd said he was smart and strong. "Why?" he asked hesitantly. "Why would you do all this for me, Nancy?" He wanted to believe he knew the answer, but the world in which he'd lived had taught him never to trust, never to hope.

"Oh, Everett," she said. "If you don't know the answer to that, then you really do need counseling." She smiled then, and as his heart swelled with hope, she pressed her lips to his briefly. "So would you go?"

"I guess so." It couldn't hurt, and maybe it could

even help. And maybe, just maybe, Nancy wouldn't leave him. "If you'll go along."

"Of course I'll go along," she said, as if that had never been in question. "I'll be right beside you."

# Nine

Sydney called her mother to tell her to expect her for dinner and declined the invitation to spend the night. After the emotional upheavals she'd endured for the past few days, all she really wanted was to bring Nick home and nestle into their snug little apartment together. Much as she loved her parents, she needed some time with her son. Just her son.

*Only he's not my son,* she reminded herself. She decided to wait until after the results of the DNA test to tell her family the unwelcome news. She was absolutely certain, deep in her heart, that Nick had been born Noah Crosby, but until she had it confirmed there was no sense in upsetting everyone. There would be plenty of time to be upset later.

It took just under an hour to make the drive north to her childhood home in Longview, Washington. She had barely gotten her car parked in her parents' driveway when the door flew open and a small figure hurtled toward her. "Mommy!"

"Nick." She scrambled out of the car and knelt with her arms wide. Her heart felt as though it was going to explode with love as her son's small body barreled into her embrace. Nick wrapped his arms around her neck as she held him close and rocked from side to side.

"I missed you, Mommy," his little voice announced from where he'd buried his face in her shoulder.

"I missed you, too, buddy," she said, dropping a kiss on the crown of his head and his straight, corn-silk-colored hair. She drew back to smile at him. "It's good to be home."

"We're not home," Nick said with irrefutable five-year-old logic as he pushed out of her arms. "We're at Gramma's house. But Gramma says we're going home after dinner."

"Gramma's right." She stood and smiled as her son went flying back up the driveway to inform his Gramma that he needed to put his suitcase in the car.

Her father had come out as well, and he chuckled. "That boy has ants in his pants," he said.

"Was he good?" She really hadn't talked to her mother long enough to hear much while she'd been away.

"Terrific," her father assured her. "I took him fishing on the Catawah twice and he caught a few under-size summer-run steelhead. I had to explain a couple of times why he couldn't keep them."

They chuckled together as they walked toward the house.

"So," her father said. "Tell me about your vacation."

Sydney squirmed. "You and Mom should go to Hawaii sometime, Daddy," she said to divert him. "It's incredibly beautiful. I saw everything I wanted, except the volcanoes on the Big Island."

"That's for another trip, hmm?" her father said as he held the door.

"Maybe sometime." She gave him a smile, hoping it didn't look as brittle as it felt. Given the finality with which Danny had let her know she couldn't be a part of his life, she doubted she'd ever voluntarily go near the island chain again.

Her mother had invited her siblings and their families for dinner, and Sydney was grateful for the whole noisy crew. Between them and Nick chattering away about everything he'd done with Gramma and Granddad while she was on "'cation," she wasn't required to do much but answer general questions about her time away.

After the meal, Nick's eyelids were drooping and she didn't linger. After all-around goodbyes and thank-yous to her parents for keeping him, she bundled her son into the car for the drive back down to their home in Portland. As she'd expected, Nick slept most of the way. He must have played hard at his grandparents' because he never even woke up when she unbuckled him from his car seat and carried him in to bed.

She slipped off his sneakers and play clothes, gave his face and hands, elbows and knees a cursory washing and got him into his pajamas, all without rousing him to more than the occasional mumble.

As she was walking back out to the garage to get the rest of their things from the car, her telephone rang. She backtracked and checked the caller ID, but it was a number she didn't recognize and the caller wasn't identified. Clicking on the phone, she said, "Hello?"

"Hi, Sydney. It's Danny."

He wouldn't have had to tell her. She'd know that voice anywhere. Funny, she thought, it was just another male voice, albeit one with a deep, pleasant tone, and yet it had the power to make her stomach lurch and her heart beat faster.

Swallowing the nerves that rose immediately, she said, "Hello, Danny."

"How was your trip up to your parents'?"

"Fine, thanks. Nick had a great time with them while I was away."

"Good."

There was a brief, awkward silence and she wondered why he had called. Surely not to engage her in this small talk. "Is there something you need?" she finally asked.

"Uh, no," he said. "I just wanted to tell you that we

should know the results of the DNA testing the day after tomorrow. Would you like to meet me at the doctor's office? That way we can both hear the results and ask any questions we have at that time."

"That would be fine." She retrieved a pencil and notepad from a nearby drawer and wrote down the address he gave her. Then there was another silence. "Danny?" she said when he didn't speak.

"Yes?"

"Would you like to come over for dinner tomorrow evening?"

"No," he said hastily. "Thanks but I already have plans."

It was exactly what she'd expected, and she'd been stupid even to set herself up for another rejection. But she hadn't been able to prevent the words from jumping out of her mouth even though she'd known as she spoke them that he'd refuse. Still, it hurt.

"All right," she said softly. "Thanks for calling."

"You're welcome." He still didn't hang up.

Finally, she said, "Danny, was there something else?"

He exhaled so heavily she heard it through the receiver. "No."

"All right. Good night." This time she didn't wait, but gently turned off the handset and put it back in the cradle. Her heart ached for him. By his own choice, he was determined to be alone. To stay alone.

And because of that, her heart also ached for herself. Something about Danny called to her, stirred her heart to wanting him, to caring for him. To loving him.

Long after she'd unpacked and gotten into bed after checking on Nick one last time, she lay awake staring at the ceiling. Reliving the days on the island before she'd remembered why she was there. The attraction, the feelings, hadn't been all on her side.

She wasn't sure how it had happened, but in just a few short days, she'd fallen in love with a man who was probably among the Top Ten Most Complicated Men in the Western Hemisphere.

And she was pretty sure that he would never allow himself to love her back.

The following day crawled by, one excruciating minute at a time. Danny spent most of it at Crosby Systems with Trent. His brother cleared out an office so that Danny could do much of the work he usually did from home. Trent had been beyond surprised when Danny had shown up in his office, but had quickly masked it and warmly welcomed him. Danny figured Trent saw his visit as another sign of his emotional stability.

Several times he nearly blurted out the whole story, nearly told his brother about Sydney and the child she seemed so certain was Noah. But something held his tongue. It wasn't simply that he wanted to protect Trent from the same heartache he was going through, although that certainly was a factor.

But there was something more. Something inside him that told him not to voice even a whisper of hope that Noah might still be alive. He couldn't be. Not after all this time.

*But what about the heart surgery?*

*Coincidence.* It had to be. Surely there were a number of adopted boys in the country who'd had heart surgery.

But not little boys whose adoptions had come about in such an unorthodox manner. Not little boys who had literally been dropped on their mothers' doorsteps at a year of age with no birth certificate and only shadowy knowledge of their pasts.

Trent invited him for dinner that evening to meet his new wife, Rebecca. Their sister Katie and her husband, Peter Logan, were coming, and Katie was dying to see him, he told Danny. But the last thing he wanted to do right now was pretend there was nothing wrong in front of his far-too-perceptive brother and sister.

Peter Logan. The thought of a member of the Logan family jarred him into thinking about his childhood friend Robbie. The older brother Peter had never even met. Robbie—Everett Baker now—had fired his public defender, Trent had told him, but Terrence Logan had hired the best criminal defense lawyers he could find to represent the son he'd just found again. Robbie hadn't wanted to accept, apparently feeling that he should be punished.

And he should. The part of Danny that was the father of a kidnapped child got furious every time he thought of Robbie involved in a kidnapping scheme, of all things. How could he? True, they'd heard that Robbie had been brainwashed until he'd forgotten his true identity, and Trent had told him some pretty sad stories about Robbie's life after he was taken. But *how could he have stolen other people's babies?*

Then a truly terrible thought occurred to him. Robbie couldn't have had anything to do with Noah's kidnapping, could he? There would be too much irony in that to be believed. He'd ascribed his son's loss to that cosmic payback theory for so long that he was stunned to think it really could be true. He'd failed to save Robbie from being snatched, and years later, Robbie might have helped snatch Danny's very own child. The thought was so disturbing that he couldn't hide his disquiet when Trent stuck his head in the door shortly before six.

"Hey," he said to Danny. "You sure you won't come to dinner?"

Danny shook his head. "Give Katie a kiss for me. And Rebecca, too." He forced a smile. "But you don't have to kiss Peter."

Trent studied his younger brother for a moment. "Something's wrong. What?"

Danny huffed out a breath of exasperated amusement at his brother's perceptiveness. He wasn't ready to talk about it. "Trent, get over yourself. You've been taking care of the rest of us for so long that you've forgotten you don't have to anymore."

Trent raised an eyebrow and looked at Danny with challenge in his eyes. "Don't I?"

"I can take care of myself."

"I don't doubt that," Trent said quietly. "But something's bothering you. All I'm offering is a sounding board if you need one."

"I don't." Slowly, Danny spoke again. "But I was wondering about something. Did you ever hear anything about the people Robbie—Everett Baker—was working with?"

Trent nodded. "One was a guy from Russia. Vladmir Kosanisky, I believe. And he's going to jail for a long, long time, thanks to Robbie's testimony. But the brains behind the whole scheme, the one they called the Stork, the guy who recruited them both, was named Charlie Prescott."

Danny shook his head. "Doesn't ring any bells."

"I don't think it should."

"Why would he do that? Steal babies?" *Cause a lifetime of anguish for the families left behind?*

"Funny you should ask." Trent hitched up his pants leg and settled on the edge of Danny's desk. "When I talked to Katie earlier, she said Peter's parents had just learned some new information from the cops. Apparently this Prescott was an orphan himself. He lived at the orphanage years before it became Children's Connection and everything it is today."

"So? Being an orphan shouldn't warp somebody that badly. Didn't he get adopted?"

"He did. But the people who adopted him must not have been screened very carefully. The father abused the boy in every way you can think of," he added soberly. "And the mother apparently did nothing to stop it. Prescott ran away when he was sixteen but he never forgot the agency that handed him over to those monsters. He went to Children's Connection a couple of years later to find out who his real parents were, but they wouldn't release the records to him."

"They couldn't, unless the biological parents had authorized it, right?"

"Right. Anyway, my guess is that was the last straw. He went over whatever cliff of decency he'd been clinging to and decided to take revenge on the agency." Trent cocked his head. "Danny! You don't think Prescott and Robbie Logan might have had something to do with Noah's kidnapping, do you? My God!" His whole body sagged. "Could that be true?"

Danny shrugged. "The only way to know is to ask Robbie."

"My God," Trent repeated. Then he glanced at his watch. "Listen, I have to go, but tomorrow, we'll make some calls, I promise. We'll find out if there's anything to this."

"I, uh, I'm tied up tomorrow morning," Danny said. "I might make it in sometime in the afternoon, though."

"What's going on?"

Danny squirmed beneath his brother's intent gaze. "Maybe nothing. I'll tell you about it later." *Maybe.* If he could manage to talk about this whole Nick Aston thing at all, it would be Trent to whom he could talk.

Trent stood. "All right. But I'm not going to forget about this."

"Like that's ever going to happen," Danny said, only half-joking.

Trent smiled, sketching a salute as he headed out the door. "See you tomorrow. We'll talk more then."

It sounded as much like a threat as it did like a promise, but Danny couldn't work up any annoyance. Trent was the glue that had held Danny's life together during its worst, blackest moments. He'd been equally involved in Katie's and Ivy's lives, far more of a parent to their younger sisters than either of their parents.

Which was a blessing. Sheila Crosby had never cared for any of her children as much as she'd cared for herself. And Jack, their dad had been so desperate to get away and stay away from Sheila that he'd left the kids to her tender mercies far too often. Oh, well. Water under the bridge. His last counselor had said he could let them continue to ruin his life or he could let it go. He chose the latter.

Deliberately, he cast thoughts of his past from his mind. He got to his feet, checking his watch and seeing that it was past time for him to leave. He was finished here for the day. Time to head back to his hotel and stare at the tube for the rest of the evening until he could sleep.

And then it would be tomorrow. The day of reckoning. The day Sydney had to face the fact that she was wrong about Nick being Noah.

He couldn't be wrong. Because deep in his heart, Danny knew his little boy was no longer alive.

He was up well before the sun the following morning, and then he had to kill hours and hours before 9:00 a.m., when he was supposed to meet Sydney at the office of the doctor who would be explaining the test results.

He was early, of course. But only moments after he took a seat in the waiting room, Sydney walked through the door. She looked cool and lovely in a pale butter-colored sweater set and flowered skirt, her face still glowing with the color she'd acquired at his home.

With her was a slender, blond-haired preschooler.

Danny felt his heart literally stop for a moment. *Knock it off!* He told himself. *That's not Noah.* Maybe not, but he couldn't keep from studying every inch of the child.

"Hello, Danny." Sydney came right over and sat down next to him. The little boy came with her, boosting himself onto a wooden chair next to hers while she set down a backpack at his feet. "Danny, this is Nicholas," she said to Danny. Turning to the boy, she said, "Nick, this is Mr. Crosby. Can you say hello?"

"Hi." The little boy smiled shyly, but his blue eyes were direct and open. "Are you a friend of my mommy's?"

"Yes," Sydney answered for him. "He is. Nick, we may have to wait awhile. I brought along a few of your books, your CD player with the new Veggie Tales CD and a couple of other things. You can decide what you want to do."

As the little boy dove into the treasures his mother had packed, Danny tried not to stare. Even though he'd known Sydney was a mother, it was odd seeing her in this new role. And he found it impossible to prevent his gaze from straying to the child over and over again, cataloging him against Danny's memories.

Sydney's son had a neatly trimmed wealth of shining hair as blond as the silk tassel on an ear of corn. Felicia's hair had been almost that color. And he'd seen pictures of himself as a small child with hair almost the same. It was still blond, still wavy, almost thirty years later, though it had darkened considerably from that early lightness.

He shifted uncomfortably. Coincidence. Besides, Noah hadn't had hair that color. Of course, Noah hadn't even had hair. It had been quite a source of amusement to Danny and Felicia when their firstborn had remained as bald as an egg month after month. When he'd turned a year old, he'd just begun to get a fringe of light fuzz around the back of his head, like an old man who'd lost it all but that small remnant.

The unexpected memory nearly undid him and to his horror, he realized he was on the verge of tears. Fiercely he fisted his hands, letting his nails bite deeply into his palms to divert his thoughts. The lump that had risen in his throat dissolved fraction by minute fraction, and the stinging in his eyes eased as well.

While he was trying to get himself under control, Nick Aston chose a book from the backpack and gave it to his mother. "Will you read this to me?" he asked her.

Sydney smiled, hefting him onto her lap. "Of course I will. And if you know any of the words as I go along, you can read them out loud, okay?"

"Okay!" It was obvious that this was a frequent activity for the pair.

Again, his gaze was drawn to the child. He seemed skinny, but Danny really didn't know a lot about kids this age. Maybe they burned a lot of energy. Or maybe it had something to do with the surgery he'd had. Would that affect his size? Logic told him probably not, unless it had truly stunted his growth, and Nick seemed tall for five. Five-and-a-half, if Sydney was right about him being a year old when he'd come to her.

Needing heart surgery. Another coincidence.

"Mr. Crosby? Ms. Aston? Dr. Cantoni will see you now." The woman in the lab coat who'd opened the inner office door smiled as she beckoned to them.

Danny stood and moved forward, aware that Sydney had stooped to help Nick gather his toys. He didn't look back, wouldn't let himself look back as he followed the woman to the end of the hallway and into a large, pleasantly appointed office in pale greens and creams. He'd spoken to the doctor on the phone but hadn't met him when he'd gone to Portland General for the lab test, and he tried to smile as the tall, thin man came forward and shook his hand. "Have a seat," he suggested, and Danny obediently sat in one of the large wing chairs.

The doctor moved around him to welcome Sydney. He also knelt to meet Nick, who let himself be led to a child-size table in front of a huge fish tank along the far wall.

"My granddad and me catched fish when I stayed wif him," Nick announced to the doctor.

The doctor snapped his fingers. "I don't have any fishing poles here. I guess you'll just have to look at these fish. I have some pretty ones in there."

Nick giggled, a happy-child sound that tore at Danny's heart all over again. "You can't catch fish in a tank!" he explained. "Only in a river. Or maybe a ocean or a lake." He looked at his mother for confirmation.

Sydney smiled and nodded. "That's right, buddy." She unzipped the backpack and set it on the floor beside the table. "Mr. Crosby and I need to talk with Dr. Cantoni for a few minutes, honey. You can play here until it's time to go." With a whoop, the little boy all but plastered his nose against the fish tank, raptly watching its inhabitants.

Sydney smiled wryly. "I'll have to drag him out of here when we're done. He's got a thing for fish."

As Sydney came forward and sat to his left, Danny took a deep breath and tried to unlock tightly clenched muscles, to relax his shoulders, to sit back in the chair rather than sitting on the edge with his hands gripped tightly together. This was it.

The doctor went around behind his desk. He opened a folder before him. "All right," he said. "Mr. Crosby, this test was performed on hair samples from you and Ms. Aston's son to determine whether that child could be your biological offspring." He took a piece of paper from the folder and slid it across the desk facing them.

"This is a chart of your DNA sequence, and below it is the child's."

He spent several moments explaining how the test was performed, how they achieved results, why those results could be considered conclusive evidence without a doubt, and then went into a detailed comparison of the two sets of test results. Halfway through, Danny realized he couldn't absorb one more word.

"Dr. Cantoni." He laid his hand in the middle of the piece of paper, obscuring the information. "Can you just tell us? Is he my son?"

The doctor stopped. He looked over his glasses at first Danny, then at Sydney. "Yes," he said. "There is no doubt in my mind, Mr. Crosby, that Nicholas Aston is your son."

*Nicholas Aston is your son…is your son…is your son.*

He heard someone gasp aloud, and realized distantly that it had been himself. The doctor was still talking, but it was only background noise to the clamor inside his head. Noah was alive. Alive! How could it be? Was he sure it wasn't a mistake? No, of course not. DNA didn't lie. That was the whole reason they'd had the test done. He became aware that there were tears on his cheeks and he put a hand to the bridge of his nose, pinching it tightly as if that would somehow stop the emotion flooding through him.

"…give us a few minutes, Dr. Cantoni? This has been a shock for Mr. Crosby." Sydney, he realized, was trying to give him time to pull himself together as she extended her hand and firmly shook the doctor's.

"Certainly. Just have my nurse call me when you're ready to continue." The doctor stood and left the room.

A moment later, Sydney's hip bumped his shoulder as she perched herself on the arm of his chair. Her right arm came around his shoulder, rubbing his upper arm gently while her other hand came down over his. She didn't say a word, but he couldn't stop himself from turning his hand over and gripping hers.

Across the room, Nick—Noah!—was chattering happily at a large purple fish with a wide mouth, apparently oblivious to the drama unfolding near the desk.

Finally, Sydney leaned down and spoke near his ear. "Danny, are you okay? Is there someone you'd like me to call?"

"No." One of the few things he did know was that he wasn't ready to share this with his family yet. "No calls." He heaved a sigh. "I'm sorry for doubting you."

She made a small, dismissive sound. "I don't blame you. You would have been foolish not to," she said, "especially after the disappointments you've had before. You must have been terrified to let yourself hope."

He swallowed and nodded. "I was so afraid it couldn't be true…."

Silence fell, broken only by the sound of the little boy's lilting voice as he continued to chatter at the fish.

As Danny sat up a little straighter, Sydney returned to her own chair. "I guess," she said softly, "we have to decide how to handle this now."

Danny glanced at her, seeing for the first time that there were tears in her eyes, too. And for the first time he realized what this news meant. He might have found his son, but Sydney would be losing hers. God! Could he do that to her?

"I don't know," he said honestly. "I need to sort out my feelings before we talk any more about what to do next." He hesitated. "Could I come over and visit him?"

Sydney squared her shoulders. "Of course. But would you mind if we don't tell Ni—him right away? I have to talk to my family first. I don't want him blurting it out to them the next time his Gramma calls."

He hadn't missed her hesitation over the boy's name. Another quandary to be resolved. And her family... This was going to require a lot more planning than he'd originally considered. It was going to affect a lot more people than simply Sydney and him, though they would be the ones to absorb the most direct impact.

Now that his mind had begun to function again, it seemed to be racing at a mile a minute. There were millions of things, it seemed, to think about. And of all of them, the only one he could positively say he was sure of right now was that he wanted his son back.

# Ten

Nick chattered all the way home about the fish. Sydney was grateful that all she had to do was mutter the occasional "Oh, yeah?" and he kept right on going. Tears ran down her face behind the large dark sunglasses she'd donned.

What was she going to do? She'd been trying to steel herself for this eventuality since the day she'd begun to suspect that Nick might be a kidnapped child. But knowing she had someone else's son and being confronted with the reality were two very different things.

Could she really give up her child?

How could she not? He wasn't hers. He was

Danny's. He'd been stolen from Danny, and the kidnapping had had tragic results for Danny and his wife. Nick was all that Danny had left. How could she not return him?

She should have tried harder to find out exactly where Nick had come from. She'd suspected from early on that he wasn't Margo's. Why hadn't she gone to the authorities? Why had she waited after she learned Margo was dead?

Because she'd already become so attached to the grinning, blue-eyed toddler that she couldn't bear to lose him. She'd been very afraid that he would be returned to someone who didn't deserve him. Someone who wouldn't ensure that his heart condition received the very best repair available, someone who wouldn't cuddle him and sing to him at bedtime or delight in his growing vocabulary and budding intellect. She'd had bad dreams about crack addicts, drug dealers, prostitutes. The reality couldn't have been further from the truth.

At the house, she managed to pull herself together. She made dinner and got Nick bathed and in bed.

And then she forced herself to pick up the telephone and call her parents. It wasn't fair to Danny to delay telling Nick about his life. And she had to tell her family before that.

Her mother cried. Her father blustered.

"But surely you can fight this in court! They can't just take your child away from you—"

"He's not my child, Daddy," she said patiently, although uttering the words aloud nearly broke her tenuous grip on her self-control. "This poor man has spent four years believing his son was dead. His wife killed herself because she couldn't face living without him. How could I possibly deny him a chance at happiness again?"

There was a tense silence on the other end of the line. Then her father spoke again. "Ah, Sydney Leigh. My thoughtful, caring girl. You always did have a heart bigger than all the rest of us put together. You're right."

"Yes," her mother said. "It may break our hearts, but it's the right thing to do." Her voice broke, but she quickly controlled it. "Honey, would you like us to tell Stu and Shelly?"

"Oh, Mom, would you?" Sydney wasn't even going to pretend not to accept; she started to cry again. "I'm not sure I can repeat this again and again. I'd really appreciate it."

"Of course," her mother said. "We'll do anything we can to make this easier for you. Do you want us to come down?"

She thought about it. Her parents loved Nick and not spending these last days with him would be difficult for them. But Danny and Nick needed time to get to know each other. That would be difficult with other people around. "Not right now," she said cautiously. "I'll let you know as soon as I have more details. I may need you a little later."

But as Sydney hung up the phone, she knew there wasn't going to be any way to make any aspect of the situation more bearable. Crying on her mother's shoulder wasn't going to make this hurt fade.

She'd barely set down the handset when the phone rang again. Checking the caller ID, she saw an unfamiliar number, but no name listed with it. She clicked on the phone. "Hello?"

"Hello, Sydney. It's Danny." He sounded nervous and uncertain. "I was wondering if you and Nick would like to go to the zoo tomorrow. I thought it might be a good way for him to get more comfortable around me."

She nodded, then realized he couldn't see her. "Sure. That's a good idea. Where shall we meet you?"

"How about I pick you up?"

"Okay. Do you have a pencil? I can give you directions."

There was a pause. "I already know where you live."

Oh. Right. Sometimes she actually forgot that the man had so much money he was practically green. He probably had had her investigated in detail the moment he left the doctor's office today. "All right, then," she said quietly. "We'll see you tomorrow. Around nine?"

"Fine. And Sydney?"

"Yes?"

"Don't worry," he said quietly. "I'm not going to rush Nick into anything. The last thing he needs is more upheaval in his life."

*But you're going to take him away from the only mother he remembers! How can that not "upheave" his life?* Drawing a deep breath, she suppressed the visceral response. "Thank you. We'll be waiting."

When she told Nick the next morning that they were going to the zoo that day, he was ecstatic. The doorbell rang promptly at nine and he raced to answer it. But as the door swung open, Nick stopped dancing around and simply stared.

On their porch stoop was a giant skunk. At least five feet tall, it was suspended in the air by a pair of muscular male arms wrapped around its furry body.

"Wow!" Nick wasn't speechless for long. "Izzat for me?"

"Nicholas!" Sydney gave him a stern stare. "Where are your manners?"

"Sorry, Mommy." He stepped back. "You can come in."

Sydney snorted, shaking her head.

Danny set the skunk down and straightened, smiling tentatively. "Good morning."

"Hello," she said. "That's, um, interesting."

"Isn't it?" He looked down at Nick. "So who do you think this skunk is for?"

Nick glanced at his mother, not about to commit another courtesy error. "I don't know. For Mommy?"

Danny raised an eyebrow. "Do you think she'd like it?"

A crafty gleam lit the little boy's eyes. "Mommies like flowers and candy," he said hopefully.

Danny laughed. "They do, don't they? Well, then, I guess you'll just have to take this skunk."

"Yay!" Nick leaped forward and pounced on the skunk. "Thank you, thank you, thank you!"

"Mr. Crosby," Sydney prompted.

"Thank you, Mr. Crosby," Nick parroted.

Sydney said, "Why don't we put that in your room until we get back from the zoo?"

But as she reached for the enormous toy, Nick grabbed it by its striped tail and began to haul it down the hallway. "I can do it myself."

"Okay." Sydney shrugged and spread her hands, smiling at Danny. "He can do everything himself these days, if you listen to him tell it."

Danny smiled again, but she caught the wistful quality. "He's so grown up."

"He starts kindergarten in the fall," she said, picking up the caps she'd gotten out for Nick and herself, the water bottles and the backpack in which she'd packed a picnic lunch.

"This is going to take some adjustment," he confessed. "In my head, he's stuck at one year old. It's hard to process that this is the same little guy whose belly I used to tickle."

"Not if you touch his belly now," she offered, trying not to let herself think about the past. "He's horrifically ticklish right there."

Nick came clattering back toward them again, halting further conversation. "Let's go to the zoo!"

Nick sang along with *Veggie Tales* the whole way

to the zoo. She supposed that was a good thing, since neither she nor Danny appeared to have much to say. She'd shown him how to buckle Nick's car seat into the rental car he was driving, and again he looked rueful. "I've got a lot to learn."

The Oregon Zoo was only ten minutes from downtown Portland. It had been renovated just a few years earlier and Nick had several favorite exhibits.

"Dollars to dimes says he'll go for the penguins," she said as they entered the main gate.

The Peruvian penguins fascinated Nick for some reason. He could stand for hours watching them waddle around awkwardly on land, only to dive into the water and swim like wild black bullets. As she'd predicted, they were soon standing watching the penguins. There was a bench a few feet away. "We can sit over there," she said to Danny. "I guarantee our feet will be a lot happier at the end of the day if we grab every chance we can find to sit down."

"Not like five-year-old feet?" he asked, smiling as he watched his son.

"Most definitely not." She settled herself on the bench and shucked off the backpack. After a moment's hesitation, she decided she might as well tackle one of the issues that was worrying her most. "Have you thought about his name?" she asked Danny, carefully not looking at him. "If you want to call him Noah again, we'll have to get him used to it."

"I did think about that last night," he admitted. "Along with about a hundred million other things." His voice was low. "Noah was Felicia's choice. I'm not particularly attached to it. And I'm afraid that changing his name would be difficult for him. Changing his last name will be enough of an adjustment."

"True." She fought to keep her voice steady. "When are you planning on taking him?"

There was a taut silence. She watched her son avidly taking in the penguins' antics, trying to blank out the thought of Nick leaving.

"Sydney." Danny's hand came down over hers in her lap and she realized she'd made nail-shaped crescents on the back of her left hand. "I'm in no hurry to whisk him away. He needs time to get used to this change. So do we."

She nodded, blinking fiercely behind the sunglasses she'd donned. "We need to tell him soon."

Danny nodded. "I called a child psychologist yesterday and made an appointment to talk to her about how to handle that. Would you like to go with me?"

She finally looked at him, touched by the thoughtfulness behind the action. "What a good idea. I would love to."

"It's tomorrow afternoon," he said.

She made a face. "I have to go back to work tomorrow. But under the circumstances, I'm pretty sure my boss will let me take the time off."

"How did your family take it?"

She heaved a sigh. "About like you'd expect. Badly."

Danny winced. "God, I wish—"

"So do I," she interrupted. "But this is just the way it happened." She sighed. "I spent a lot of time last night wishing I had tried harder to find out who he really was four years ago."

Danny squeezed her hands again with his much larger one. "I'm sure you never could have imagined anything as crazy as this. Let's stop looking back and just look forward."

"All right." But she wasn't sure why. All she had to look forward to was an empty house.

"Who keeps Nick while you work?" he asked, removing his hand.

"A lady on the next floor," she said. "He goes to a private preschool two days a week also."

"I was thinking…would it be possible for me to baby-sit while you're working? It would be a great way for the two of us to get to know each other."

"You?" She couldn't resist the startled laugh. It seemed ridiculous to expect a member of one of the city's wealthiest families to act as her baby-sitter. "I suppose so. If you really want to."

"I want to," he said firmly.

Just then Nick came tearing across the macadam to the bench. "Can we go see the blowhole now, Mommy?"

Danny said, "The what?" and Nick grinned. Danny grinned back at him.

"It's near the sea lion cove," she said. "It's a natural rock formation that shoots ocean water into the air every so often."

Both Danny and Nick turned their faces to her, still smiling. Two sets of identical blue eyes, two stubborn chins with an irresistible cleft. Two heads of blond hair, though Danny's wasn't the white-blond that his son's was.

It was shocking to see how very much the man and boy resembled each other, and she simply stared at the two of them, lost in the moment.

*My God,* she thought. *How could anyone doubt that these two are father and son?*

"Have a seat," Terrence Logan said to the private investigator, showing him to one of the wing chairs in the formal room where the Logan family received guests. Terrence and his wife, Leslie, took the loveseat directly across from their visitor. "You have a report for us?"

The man nodded. He laid a thick folder on the glass-topped table between them. "I interviewed your son first. For the sake of clarity I'm going to refer to him as Everett Baker. He was very helpful. From there I was able to track backward almost to the date he was kidnapped."

Leslie made a small, stifled sound, but she gripped her hands tightly together in her lap and pressed her lips together.

"I believe you already know the basic events," the man said. "What I've done is gone back and filled in the spaces as much as possible. I went to his old schools, neighbors, in the few cases any could be located. Even a hospital in Dayton where he was treated for a broken bone when he was eleven."

"Abuse?" Leslie almost whispered the word.

The man shook his head. "I don't know. Nothing could be proved, and the couple moved before a social worker could investigate. Twenty years ago it wasn't nearly as easy to locate people as it is today."

"So, who were they?" Terrence leaned forward. "And why did they take our son?"

"Lester and Jolene Baker were the names of the couple who took him. Those were their real names and at no time did I find any evidence that they used false identities. They first settled in Cleveland with the boy, but they moved frequently. Over the next decade, they moved back and forth at least a dozen times between Ohio, Michigan and Indiana. Everett was enrolled in school in most of those places but his attendance record was spotty and when they moved, the teachers usually had no warning. He just wouldn't show up one day and weeks later they might get a request for his records from the receiving school in the new home area."

"How could they enroll him in school without his birth certificate?" Terrence asked. "Did they forge one?"

The investigator shook his head. "No. They had a birth certificate. What no one ever realized was that they also had a death certificate. The Bakers had a son the same year your son Robbie was born. He was named Everett, but he died of Sudden Infant Death

Syndrome a few months after birth." The man cleared his throat. "At least, that's what your son was told. He says that over the years he came to suspect that Mrs. Baker may have accidentally killed the child. Apparently she wasn't the most stable person in the world."

Leslie shuddered and put a hand to her throat. Terrence's face was frozen into a carefully blank expression, but he reached over and put an arm around his wife's shoulders.

The P.I. looked back down at the notes he'd extracted from the folder. "When Everett—your son—was sixteen, Lester Baker abandoned the family. Everett intended to run away as well, but his mother—"

"She was *not* his mother," Leslie said in a steely voice at odds with her usual gentle demeanor.

"Right." The P.I. continued, correcting himself. "Mrs. Baker attempted suicide. She was hospitalized and apparently Everett never felt he could leave her again. He finished high school and got a job, then put himself through a community college by taking classes at night for the next six years. When he got his degree, he got a job in Missouri and both he and Mrs. Baker moved to St. Louis. She died there in 2001. She had liver cancer. Before she died, Everett found the death certificate I mentioned earlier among her things. Of course, that led him to suspect he wasn't her son. When he confronted her, she told him the whole story."

"Four years ago? But why didn't he look for us then?" Leslie asked.

"He did, after a fashion," the P.I. replied. "After

Mrs. Baker's death, he moved to Portland, where he got a job in the accounting department of Children's Connection, which he had learned you were deeply involved with."

"So close..." Terrence murmured. "Four years wasted."

"Mr. Logan, Mrs. Logan, I don't believe Everett felt he could approach you at that point. He'd done research on you and your family. He knew you'd buried a child you believed was him, and that you'd had other children. He has an enormous amount of guilt—"

"Guilt? Whatever for?" Leslie asked.

"He believes he let you down. He thinks he should have tried harder to get away the day he was taken, and that he should have been smart enough to avoid being snatched at all. He can't forgive himself for forgetting his past."

"He was *six*," Terrence said forcefully. "Just a little boy. We never blamed him in any way."

"I know that," the man said. "But you must understand. Your son was raised by two people who were verbally abusive, at the very least. From things I read in some of the school reports, I suspect it went further than that, though he's never confirmed it. Initially, I believe he was brainwashed. They told him you didn't want him back. For some time he felt that you'd quit on him. Now that this all has come out, he feels as if he quit on you."

"That couldn't be more wrong," Leslie said softly. "I want to tell him that myself."

"So how did he get mixed up in this trouble?" Terrence asked.

The private investigator glanced at his notes again. "In Portland, Everett was approached by a man named Charlie Prescott—"

"The one who was killed recently."

"Yes. Prescott already had kidnapping plans in mind, as well as other things, and I believe he recruited Everett because he seemed like an easy mark. Your son was moved around too much to make friends during his formative years. He was—still is—almost painfully withdrawn with most people. He was lonely. Prescott offered him something that must have been irresistible—friendship."

"And from there he talked him into helping with his plans." Terrence rubbed his forehead. "Poor Robbie."

The P.I. nodded. He tapped the folder, then slid it across the table. "In here are all the details of his education from his school records. I also spoke with some of Lester Baker's employers in various locations, as well as employees at the St. Louis hospital at which Mrs. Baker died, and Everett's co-workers in St. Louis and here in Portland. He's formed a relationship with a young woman, a nurse. I also spoke to her. She seems pleasant, honest and very self-confident. I sense that they're quite close."

"Nancy Allen." Terrence smiled slightly. "She called and thanked me after I posted his bail bond. I want to meet her one of these days."

"Yes." The investigator stood. "I'll leave the

information with you. Just call if there's anything else I can do for you."

"Thank you so much. We're glad to have anything that can help us understand Robbie better." Terrence stood as well and offered a hand. "Why don't you come over to my office and we'll settle your bill right now?"

As Terrence ushered the man from the room, Leslie picked up the folder and began to read.

# *Eleven*

If Danny ever had been so nervous about anything in his life, he couldn't remember it. He knew nothing about five-year-old boys except that he'd been one once. And that year of his life had been the last happy one before a disastrously difficult childhood that in very few ways could be called normal.

Danny took a deep breath as he stood in front of Sydney's door, listening to small footsteps come pounding toward the door. He couldn't afford to screw up this chance to begin to bond with his son.

"Hi, Mr. Crosby! Did you bring stuff to play with?" His son stood in the open doorway, with a grin wide enough to split his little face.

"Uh, no," he said. Hell. He was already striking out.

"That's okay," Nick consoled him. "You can play with mine."

"Thanks." Amused and vastly relieved that he hadn't failed some test, Danny gestured toward the interior of the house. "May I come in?"

"Oh! Yeah." Nick turned and started to march toward the living room, leaving Danny to enter and shut the door. "Mommy gets mad usually when I answer the door without her. But today she said I could."

"I guess it's not a good idea to talk to strangers when Mommy's not around."

"Uh-uh." The little blond head shook back and forth emphatically. "'cuz they might steal me."

Danny had to shut his eyes for a moment against a sudden surge of emotion. His son had been too little to learn that lesson four years ago. How ironic that Sydney had done such a good job of teaching it.

But then he thought of Robbie, walking away with the strange man, despite having been taught not to talk to strangers. It was far too easy to tempt a child of this age, Danny knew. A parent would never be able to relax his vigilance. Once again, he gave a silent "thank you" to whatever fate had led Nick into Sydney's arms. Robbie's life had been changed in much the same way, but the experience apparently had been much different.

When he opened his eyes, Sydney was standing at the kitchen doorway. Her blue eyes were sober and sympathetic. "Is this going to be all right?" she asked him. Not because she doubted his ability to care for his son, he realized, but because she was concerned that it would be too hard on *him*.

The knot around his heart loosened. He nodded. "Yeah. It will." As his nerves died away and her appearance began to register, he realized how lovely she looked in a midnight-blue business suit that hugged her slender figure. The skirt stopped just above her knees, revealing the legs he found so attractive in flirty, slender heels. The delicate white sweater beneath the jacket was just sheer enough to show a hint of lace beneath. "You look great," he said. "Pretty."

She smiled. "Thank you. 'Pretty' wasn't exactly what I was going for but I'll take it."

"What were you going for?" He raised an eyebrow. "Believe me, Sydney, you're going to have to work a whole lot harder than that to escape looking pretty."

She blushed. Blushed! Her whole *pretty* face went rosy.

"Hey, Mr. Crosby! Wanna play Nintendo with me?" Nick's piping voice interrupted a moment that was quickly growing too intense, too intimate, for the casual relationship they'd adopted since returning to Portland.

"He can play in a minute, honey," Sydney said. "First let me show him a few things." She turned and led the way into the kitchen, where she pointed at the front of the refrigerator. "There's a list here with essential information—my work number and mobile phone, my e-mail, Nick's personal information and doctor's name and number. Right at this moment my mother and father are listed as his next of kin but obviously that's changed. We can take care of that paperwork this week." Her voice was brisk and unemotional, though he knew how difficult this whole situation was for her. Yesterday he'd watched her struggle with tears more than once. "There are sandwiches, cut-up watermelon and a jar of carrots and celery in the frig for lunch. For snacks there are apples, bananas, crackers and peanut butter. Don't let him talk you into cookies."

He smiled. He'd bet his island the subject of cookies would come up after she left. "Would it be okay if I took him to a park or something?"

She nodded. "There's a great neighborhood park two blocks over. Nick can get you there. Around eleven, there's an informal play group that shows up. It's a nice chance for him to hang with some other kids for a little bit." She spread her hands. "He's really not a lot of work if you have the time to play with him. What else do you want to know?"

He thought for a moment, but she seemed to have pretty well covered everything. "I think I can wing it from here," he said. Then something occurred to him. "Is it all right if he calls me Danny?"

She nodded slowly. "But…don't you want him to call you Daddy? Should we see what the counselor tells us this afternoon?"

Danny shrugged. "Danny's not much of a stretch from Daddy when the time comes to talk to Nick. And it feels weird to have him calling me Mr. Crosby. Mr. Crosby is my father."

Sydney smiled. "All right."

They made arrangements to meet at the counselor's office late that afternoon. He'd take Nick to his regular baby-sitter first so they could speak freely.

But as he and Nick walked outside to wave goodbye when Sydney climbed into her car, a dark-haired man came out of the apartment next door. He wore a T-shirt and cut-off athletic shorts and Danny could see muscles the size of footballs in his arms as he went down the steps toward her car. "Hey, Syd! Glad you're back."

Danny couldn't hear her reply but he saw her roll down her window and lean an elbow out of the car as she smiled up at the guy.

"Who's that?" he asked Nick shamelessly.

"Erran. He's our neighbor."

"The one who helped you build your go-cart?"

Nick nodded. "Yeah. Erran's cool."

Cool, huh? It didn't make Danny like the guy any better. In fact, if he touched Sydney's arm like that one more time, Danny might have to go over there and rip off a couple of fingers. And her name was not Syd.

*Sydney's not yours,* he reminded himself. *You're not looking for a woman.* Just getting his son back was enough for him.

Wasn't it?

The day went well, in his estimation. Nick accepted him easily, chatting away about the minutiae of his young life.

"Where do you live?" he asked after Danny told him he'd have to see Danny's home one day.

"I live in Hawaii. I have to take a plane ride to get there. And then a boat ride because I live on an island."

Nick's eyes were enormous. "That sounds far."

Danny nodded. "I guess it is."

"An island has water all around it."

"Right. And it's warm all the time on my island. I can go swimming any time I want."

"Do you take your kids swimming?"

The innocent question sliced deeply. When he responded, he chose his words carefully. "I don't have any children who live with me. Just two people who take care of my house, Leilani and Johnny."

"Leilani and Johnny." Nick rolled the words around on his tongue a couple of times, giggling. "Hey, that rhymes! That means they sound alike."

"You are too smart for me, buddy." He realized a second later that he'd used Sydney's special nickname for her son. But Nick didn't seem to mind. "Maybe," he added casually, "you can meet them someday if you visit my house."

"Cool!" Apparently everything in his young life was cool. He smiled as Nick muttered, "Leilani and Johnny," again, still grinning.

The counseling appointment that afternoon started out well enough. The psychologist was a woman, and she listened carefully to each of them as they told the story of Nick's life. She was circumspect, but Danny could see she was pleased that he wasn't insisting they tell Nick who he really was that very afternoon, or anything quite so rash.

Then Danny asked how long she thought they should wait before moving him.

"It would be best to let him absorb the change in his family structure before you change his living environment. Perhaps you could talk to him about his father before there's any mention of moving." She steepled her fingers and looked over them at Danny. "I presume he'll eventually live with you again, Mr. Crosby?"

"Yes." That was one thing he was sure of.

"And how far away from his current home will you be living?"

"I'm planning on taking him back to Hawaii," said Danny.

"But what about school?" Sydney interrupted. "You'll have to take him over to Kauai every day!"

"I'd thought about getting a tutor. Someone to live in."

Her eyebrows rose and he could see she didn't like it. "But what about playmates? You can't expect him to be as solitary as you are, Danny. He's used to going to preschool with other kids. He plays soccer. How is he going to do that on the island?" Her voice rose slightly.

Before he could respond, the counselor said, "I can see that this is an issue that needs to be decided before we explore your options further. Why don't you revisit it in a day or two when each of you has had time to think about it, and next week we can talk about how best to prepare Nick for whatever impact the final decision will have on his life?"

"There's no need to revisit it," Sydney said, and her whole demeanor was different. Shut down, contained. Her voice was very quiet now, very subdued. "Mr. Crosby is Nick's parent. He'll be making those decisions. My role is simply to prepare Nick as best I can for whatever is going to happen."

The counselor looked at her impassively. "Is it really that cut and dried? You've raised this child, been his mother since he was tiny. The thought of losing him must be devastating."

"Well, of course it is!" There was heat in Sydney's voice again. "But Danny didn't give up his son voluntarily. It's not like he signed off on his parental rights when I adopted Nick. I can't…won't stand in his way now that he's found him." Her voice trembled. "Yes, the thought of waking up and going through each day without that precious little person is tearing me up inside, but what do you expect me to do? He was stolen from his parents. He's not mine to give back." And she started to cry.

No, not cry. Sob. Hard. As if her heart would break. As if it *was* breaking.

Danny was stunned. Sydney had been so controlled, so calm about all this. Oh, he'd seen her cry, seen how difficult it was for her to talk about it, but until he'd seen this passionate outburst, he hadn't really let himself acknowledge what was going to happen. No, that wasn't right. What *he* was going to do. To her.

The counselor let Sydney's words hang in the air for a long moment.

Danny reached over and put a hand on Sydney's back, feeling helpless and guilty. Her body was warm and slender beneath his hand, quivering with the sobs that shook her, and for the first time in a long time, fury rose at the person who'd kidnapped Nick so long ago. He'd spent a lot of time that first year being furious. After Felicia's death, though, it had seemed like too much effort to be angry. It was easier just not to care.

Now there was a whole new component of this to deal with. It wasn't just him, not just Felicia, any longer. Now Sydney and her whole family were going to go through the devastation of losing a child, too.

Sydney fumbled in her purse and withdrew a small pack of tissues, and Danny let his hand slide away. He almost wanted to smile. She was so organized, so efficient. He could have predicted there would be tissues in there.

She wiped her eyes and blew her nose and sat back in her chair. "Sorry," she said in Danny's direction, though she didn't meet his eyes.

He wished he had the right to put his arm around her again, to comfort her until she felt better. But he didn't. And the one thing that would make her feel better was something he couldn't give her.

His son.

He couldn't let himself get involved with Sydney,

he told himself fiercely. No matter how badly he wanted her, she deserved someone better. She didn't need someone like him, someone too...damaged to feel all the things she wanted him to feel. She needed a nice, normal guy who would give her a nice, normal marriage and a bunch of nice, normal kids of her own. Not a guy who could never love again.

Finally, the psychologist spoke again. "Have you two discussed setting up some sort of visitation arrangement? This situation is not unlike that of divorcing parents where the custodial parent is moving the child some distance away. And it certainly would be healthier for the child than having his mother suddenly disappear from his life. No matter how well you prepare him, that's going to impact him negatively."

Visitation. He'd never even considered it. Danny could feel words of protest rising, but he squashed them before they could leak out. He'd been without his son for four years. He didn't want to live without him for even one day from now on. Did that make him selfish?

Maybe. He sighed and leaned forward, elbows on knees. "I guess I do have a lot to think about," he said slowly. He turned and looked at Sydney, sitting quietly beside him, her face a frozen, unreadable mask. "And talk about."

"Charlie used to boast," Everett said to Detective Levine, the Portland cop who was interviewing him. He'd spoken to Levine when he'd first decided to turn himself in and was marginally comfortable with the man's low-key manner. Not like the FBI agent who stood in the corner, watching him with a jaundiced eye. If Agent Delane had had his way, Everett suspected he'd have been thrown into a dungeon and Delane would have melted down the key.

But today Delane didn't intimidate him quite as much. He felt…almost courageous. And it was all due to Nancy. She sat at his side, her slender fingers laced firmly through his, and he had the sense that she was ready to pounce on Delane at the slightest provocation. She'd clearly decided Levine was the friendlier of the two and she'd pointedly ignored Delane ever since.

"Boast about what?" Levine prompted.

"He told me about a number of kidnappings he committed on his own before we met. He stole babies from wealthy couples, demanded ransoms and then didn't return the babies as he promised. He kept both the ransom and the children, then turned around and resold the kids to people who wanted to adopt."

"Making money on both ends of the deal," said the detective grimly. He rattled a piece of paper. "I have a list here of babies up and down the West Coast that vanished during the years Prescott might have been doing this. Will you look it over and see if there are any specific names he mentioned, or even if you know he was in the cities in question during those times?"

Everett nodded. "Sure. But I only know a few names. I'm sure there are at least a dozen I never heard details about. Later, when he was too afraid he'd get caught, he switched his tactics again. He started taking babies from young, usually single mothers living on welfare or just scraping by." He took the list and began to peruse it, occasionally picking up a highlighter that the detective provided and noting something that looked familiar. "You know, people who might not get as much attention from law enforcement as wealthy couples do."

The cop had the grace to wince.

"How will this help?" Nancy asked.

"We've tracked down one of the guys who used to supply Prescott with fake paperwork," the cop explained. "If Mr. Baker recognizes anything here, we may be able to match it with some of the adoptions that were made."

"You mean you'd be able to get these babies back?" Nancy's eyes lit up.

The cop looked at the federal agent. "Yeah," said Delane. "It's possible that we might find some of them. But it's going to be one unholy mess, since I'm sure a lot of them have adoptive families who love them just as much now."

"Oh my," Nancy said in dismay. "This is a big mess, isn't it?"

"You don't know the half of it."

*"Daniel Crosby?"* Nancy, the agent and the detective were brought up short by Everett's exclamation as the familiar name leaped off the page at him.

The cop looked at the name to which Everett was pointing. "Yeah. Heard of him? Crosby Systems tycoon, child abducted four years ago right here in Portland?"

"Oh, God." Everett's face was the color of the piece of paper. "Danny Crosby was my best friend. He was there the day I got taken. If this is the same man…"

Nancy had brought a hand to her lips in dismay. "Then he's endured *two* kidnappings," she said in distress. "Why did you highlight that name, Everett?"

His whole body was shaking, and he felt completely sick to his stomach. "The date and place connection. That wasn't too long before I met Charlie and I know for a fact he was operating in Portland then. But if this is the baby he snatched, it didn't go like all the others." He shook his head, concentrating to recall every detail. "He had some girlfriend at the time who ran away and took the kid and the adoptive people's money along with her. Charlie said, and this is a direct quote, 'It took me awhile but I tracked her down and fixed her ass.' He said he never found the money or the kid, though. He was pretty furious about it for a long time."

"Do you remember the woman's name?" The detective looked as if he were having a hard time staying calm.

Everett shook his head. "Mary? Marie? I don't think… *M* something, though. Margaret! No, Margo. I remember it was unusual. But I don't know a last name."

"Jesus." Delane rubbed a hand over his face. "Looks

like your pal Charlie was into more than just kidnapping."

"Margo." The cop was scribbling it down. He rose from the table and both he and the agent started from the room. "Don't worry about the last name. I think you may have given us exactly what we needed."

As the two men left the room, Nancy looked at Everett oddly. "You remember your best friend?"

The words shocked him as he realized that he did indeed remember Danny. "Yeah," he said with a touch of wonder. "I do. But half of it may be stuff I dreamed up. It's hard to say."

"Your parents could tell you," Nancy said. Her hazel eyes were steady and clear.

"I…yeah," he said. "They probably could. But I doubt they'd want to meet me now."

"Don't bet on it," she told him. "If my child had been kidnapped and found almost thirty years later, there's no power on earth that could stop me from seeing him again."

*My child…* He didn't mean to ask such a personal question, but the words popped out before he could stop them. "Do you want children someday?"

She looked into his eyes and smiled, the special smile that he'd begun to realize was only for him. "Oh, yes. Having children with the man I love would make my life just about perfect."

He nodded. But he couldn't bring himself to ask her to clarify that statement. Was it just a figure of speech, or was there someone specific she had in mind? He hoped so, more than he'd ever hoped for anything in his entire life.

And he hoped that someone was him.

Danny met Sydney at the door the following afternoon. She could see Nick at the kitchen table, happily slopping away with some water-soluble paint on butcher paper.

"Hey," he said. "How was your day?"

"Fine, thank you. How about you two?" Be friendly and polite, nothing more, she reminded herself. Danny had made it clear the day before that all he wanted was to get his son and get back to his solitary existence.

"Our day was great. I'll let Nick tell you about it. But first, I have a favor to ask."

She raised an eyebrow inquiringly. "A favor?"

"My brother, Trent, has invited us for dinner. He and his wife, Rebecca, are dying to meet Nick. They'd like you to come, too. I didn't remember you already knew them until Rebecca mentioned it. Will you come?"

She was taken aback. "But we haven't told Nick yet—"

"They know that, and they'll be circumspect." He paused. "Trent was at the hospital the day Noah was born. He paced the waiting room like it was *his* kid, and he was the first person who got to hold him after Felicia and I. He's really anxious to see him."

She couldn't say no to that. But she wanted to. Oh, she wanted to.

She didn't want to visit with members of Danny's family, even with a friend as dear as Rebecca, whose husband had memories of Nick older than her own. She just wanted to take her son and run away and hide forever.

The thought shocked her. What was she thinking? Nick had been taken from Danny once already. She could be gracious about this. She would be. "You don't really need me there at a family gathering."

"I'd like you there," Danny said quietly. "Please."

Rats. How was she supposed to resist that? Especially when those beautiful blue eyes were watching her so intently. Did he know that she had no defenses against him when he needed her? "All right. What time?"

They arrived at Trent and Rebecca's home shortly before seven. She'd given Nick a snack, since they'd be eating later than he was used to. The last thing she wanted was for him to show his cranky side.

She'd known Trent Crosby before she'd met Danny, but until she saw them together by Trent's front door she'd never thought about what a resemblance they shared. Trent was a scant inch taller than Danny and his eyes were a warm brown rather than blue. Nick had inherited the family looks, too.

Trent's eyes widened slightly the moment he saw the small boy by Sydney's side. He blinked rapidly several times and a muscle ticced in his lean jaw, and she realized he was fighting strong emotion. He cleared his throat and knelt before Nick. "Hey there," he said, extending a hand just as if Nick were fifty rather than five. "I'm Trent Crosby. What's your name?"

"Nicholas Aston," Nick said. "And this is my mommy. Her name's Sydney an' her last name's the same as mine."

Trent's lips twitched and his taut features relaxed. "That's a good thing," he pronounced. "Would you like to come in, Nicholas Aston?"

Nick giggled and his blue eyes shone as he started across the threshold. "You can call me Nick."

A slim, pretty, dark-haired woman came into view then. "Hello," she said to Danny. "I'm Rebecca. Hey, kiddo!" She knelt and hugged Nick. "How was your visit with Gramma?"

The evening went far better than Sydney had expected. Trent apparently had been excited about his nephew's visit. He'd run out to a local toy store and bought an obscene number of brand-new toys, gadgets and building sets. After a few minutes of conversation, both Trent and Danny got down on the floor and helped Nick build a detailed city with an elaborate train track running through it.

"I'll get dinner ready while the children are playing." Rebecca smiled as she stood.

"May I help?" Sydney followed her into the kitchen. Despite the fact that she and Rebecca were friends, had known each other for some time, she felt awkward and out of place now that she knew for certain these people were her son's family.

"You can put salad in those bowls, if you really want to help." Rebecca pointed toward the counter. "Or you can sit there and drink your wine and tell me all about how you broke your big news to Danny."

Sydney headed for the salad bowls. "What would you like to know?"

Rebecca laughed. "Everything." Then her brown eyes grew serious. "But I'll settle for how you're doing with all this. I can't even imagine learning that my child belongs to someone else."

"Someone who wants him back," Sydney said baldly. She sighed. "That came out badly. I don't want to deny Danny his son. I feel terrible for the years he lost, and…everything else."

Trent's wife nodded. "You mean Felicia. I never met her but Trent's told me. I guess she made Danny happy, but Trent never really cared for her. He said he always thought she seemed emotionally fragile. You do know how they met?"

Sydney nodded. "At the rehab place he went to after his suicide attempt."

Rebecca nodded. "She was there for the same reason. Only she'd tried it three times before."

Dear Lord. A recipe for disaster, Sydney thought, subjecting someone that fragile to the stress of losing a child to kidnapping. She blew out a deep, resigned breath. "One of the reasons I don't have the heart to make this difficult—more difficult—for Danny is because of what he's been through. Losing both his child and his wife in the space of a year…"

"I admire you," Rebecca said. "I couldn't do what you're doing."

"Yes, you could," Sydney began, but Rebecca shook her head.

"No. I couldn't." She took a deep breath and tears shone in her eyes. "You know what the miscarriage did to me. And to Trent. If I ever have a child of my own, I'd kill anyone who tried to take him from me." She put a hand over her mouth. "Oh, Sydney, I'm sorry. I know I'm too blunt, and this is none of my business."

"I don't mind. It's actually a relief to talk about it." Sydney gestured toward the living room. "But that's just it. Yes, I love Nick as if he was mine, but he isn't. Danny didn't choose to give him up, and it would be wrong of me to fight to keep him. And don't think I haven't thought about it," she added wistfully.

But Rebecca still was shaking her head. "I understand what you're saying. Intellectually, I even agree. But here—" she tapped the area right over her heart "—I could never let him go. If I'd raised him, I'd do anything to keep him in my life, biological claims or not."

"Hey! We've got three hungry men in here. How's the kitchen crew doing?" Trent's voice interrupted the sober moment.

"Go wash your hands," Rebecca called back. "This stuff is ready to put on the table." As she headed for the dining room with a platter of roast chicken that she'd just finished slicing, she stopped and met Sydney's gaze with compassion. "When this all gets settled, you know you can always use my ear if you need one. And my tissues," she added with a wry grimace.

# Twelve

Nick was just about asleep on his feet by the time they got home at nine-thirty. Sydney had given him a bath before they went over to Trent and Rebecca's, so all she had to do was usher him through face-washing and teeth-brushing before she bundled him into bed.

Danny watched from the doorway, but when she asked if he'd like to help, he shook his head. "You've got a system, I can tell. Some night when he's not so sleepy, I'll take a turn."

When she bent over his bed for a goodnight kiss, Nick threw his arms around her neck. "I love you, Mommy."

"I love you, too, buddy," she whispered.

Then he mumbled. "'Night, Danny. I love you."

There was a moment of electric stillness. Finally, Danny moved. He crossed the room and bent down. He touched his lips to Nick's silky blond hair. "I love you, too. See you tomorrow."

He was standing so close that when Sydney rose from the edge of the bed, their bodies brushed. But Danny didn't move, simply put his hands on her arms and held her there, her back to his front as they both looked down at the sleeping child.

Sydney closed her eyes and let herself drink in the moment. She, her son and his father, together. If only it could always be like this. Danny's hands were warm on her arms, his body big and hard where she rested against him. It wasn't hard to imagine that they were really a family.

It was that thought that made her step away. Quietly, she slipped around Danny and headed for the hallway. But she'd barely cleared the door of Nick's room when Danny stopped her by taking her arm again.

"Sydney?"

She looked down at his hand on her arm. If she looked at him now, she knew he would see her feelings reflected in her eyes. "Yes?"

"Thank you for going with me tonight. I— It was a lot easier with you there."

Now *that* was a loaded statement. She wondered if he even realized what he'd just said. Taking a deep breath, she turned and looked up at him. "Why was that?"

Danny hesitated, clearly surprised by the question. He opened his mouth, then closed it again. His shoulders slumped. "Sydney," he said quietly, "you don't want this. Me. Knowing we're both bound to Nick creates a bond—"

"—that we were feeling before I even remembered I had a son," she interrupted. If she was going to gamble, she might as well toss in all her chips. "I love you, Danny." She lifted her finger to his lips when he would have spoken again. "Shh. Let me finish. Yes, Nick is a factor in our relationship. He has to be now. But even without him, I'd still have come back from Hawaii mourning the loss of the chance of my life. The chance to be with a man I love." She put both hands up and framed his face, rubbing her thumbs over his lips, letting him see everything she was feeling in her eyes. "Will you stay tonight?"

Danny hesitated. "Sydney, I can't make any promises—"

"I know." She let her hands drop. "I'm not asking for promises. Tonight is my gift to you."

Danny closed his eyes briefly. "That's not fair," he said hoarsely. "You know what you do to me. How can you offer me this and expect me to walk away?"

Despite the ache gripping her chest, she smiled. "I don't."

Danny stood frozen for a moment, clearly a man at war with himself. Then he stepped forward and bent, sweeping her off her feet and into his arms so smoothly that she gasped and clutched at his neck. His mouth came down on hers even as he began to walk toward her bedroom, and Sydney gave herself fully to the magic that their bodies made together.

He carried her into her bedroom and set her on her feet beside the bed. Then he stepped away to turn on the little bedside lamp and pull her sheets and duvet to the foot of the bed.

As they faced each other Danny took a deep breath. "I want you," he said in a low voice. "I dream of making love to you all the time. I want it to be real."

The words seduced her as surely as any skilled touch, and she smiled. "I've dreamed of you touching me."

His eyes darkened with heat and desire and he reached for the hem of the little top she'd worn to dinner. It came up and over her head and he tossed it away. As she shook her hair free, his hands were already on the clasp of her bra, and then it, too, went flying through the air to land on the rug beside her bed. Moments later, he removed the last of her clothing when he slid her bikini panties off and tossed them onto the pile.

His gaze seared her from head to toe, so intent that she felt embarrassed, but as she lifted her arms to cross them over her torso, Danny caught them and gently held her wrists at her sides.

"I knew you were beautiful," he said seriously, and every ounce of her self-consciousness died away.

He released her then, stepping back to peel off his own shirt. He removed his pants as well, sliding out of his casual loafers at the same time and stood before her in nothing but a pair of white briefs that left little doubt about the extent of his desire for her.

He'd said she was beautiful, but he was magnificent. His chest was broad, his shoulders heavily built with muscle defining his arms. His lean thighs also were muscled, probably from the running, and his stomach was flat and ridged with strength. He wasn't hairy, but had a single line of blond hair bisecting his chest, growing wider beneath his navel before it vanished into his briefs.

A sudden wave of desire surged through her and her whole body nearly shook with the need to touch him, to slide away the cloth and see all of him. She squeezed her eyes tightly shut for a long moment, and when she opened them, he was kicking away the briefs. Stark-naked and fully aroused, he made her pulse pound and her body feel the need to shift restlessly, to assuage the jittery, needy feeling growing between her thighs.

She steeled herself for his touch, but instead he took her hand and tugged her toward the bed. Without a word, he urged her onto the crisp white expanse of the mattress. She turned onto her side, watching as he lay down beside her. His erection was cushioned in a thick cloud of blond curls, angling slightly to the side. She put out a hesitant hand and Danny reached out and met it, guiding her to him. He wrapped her fingers around the thick, heated shaft, and she heard his breath whistle out as she explored the satiny column, petting and stroking him, feeling the pulse of his heart pounding through him, filling him even more.

Again, he covered her hand with his, showing her how to lightly grip and stroke him. When she glanced up at his face, his eyes were tightly closed and there were wild spots of color high on his cheekbones. Sydney sighed with pleasure as his hips surged against her hand. She increased the speed of her strokes until with a groan, he dragged her hand away. "I don't want to come yet," he whispered. "Not just yet."

He urged her onto her back and laid his hand on her belly. She was so sensitive she flinched at the touch and he smiled as he slid his hand lower to comb through the soft curls at the V of her legs. "Spread your legs a little."

Sydney did as he asked. She was so beautiful, she made his whole body ache with the need to bury himself deep inside her. But he'd longed for this, wanted this, dreamed of it, and he refused to rush.

Slowly, he slipped his hand down and down, feeling the soft folds part to admit his index finger. She was slick and wet and so hot he just wanted to get inside her, to feel that heat and moisture surrounding him. He slid a finger deep into her and Sydney's hips lifted off the bed, shoving him deep into the silky channel. Her muscles quivered around him, and he was momentarily awed by the force of the attraction between them. He'd barely begun to touch her and yet he knew—he *knew*—that with the slightest effort he could bring her to climax.

He wanted it in the worst way, but even more, he wanted to be inside her when she came. Carefully, slowly, he withdrew his hand and reached for the small package he'd tossed onto her bedside table. Then shifting over her, he parted her legs and made a place for himself there. They both sighed when his erection was sandwiched between her legs, and she wriggled wildly beneath him, trying to push herself up high enough for him to enter her.

Danny held her back, though, enjoying her struggles. But when she reached for him again he pinned both wrists above her head with one big hand. "Oh, no," he said. "We're in this together, babe."

"Then *do it!*" she said. She lifted her head and nipped at his bottom lip. "Danny, *please.*"

He took her hips in his hands and held her in place, rearing back on his knees until his shaft was poised between her thighs. She whimpered as he moved forward just a fraction, lodging the head of his erection in her channel but not letting her have it all.

Sydney clasped his buttocks in her hands. "You tease." She was smiling into his eyes. And then she drove her heels hard into the bed and pushed herself up in one abrupt motion, and he was inside her. All the way. He gasped, and she arched her back and cried out, and around him, incredibly, he felt her begin to come, squeezing him rhythmically as her body bucked and shuddered beneath his. He felt himself draw taut, his own body rushing madly out of control, and he stopped fighting it. He let himself go, pounding roughly into her as she arched and thrust beneath him, letting himself plunge fast and hard, flesh slapping soft, responsive flesh, until with a harsh groan, he spent himself inside her, feeling the jetting pulses of release shooting into her. He collapsed on her smaller body, every ounce of energy drained from him along with the shattering climax. Sydney immediately wrapped her arms and legs around him, angling her head to kiss his jaw. Neither of them spoke.

After a few moments, he withdrew from her body. But he didn't leave, though he probably should have. Instead, he turned onto his side and drew Sydney back against him, resting his head just behind hers on her pillow. He reached down and flipped up the sheet, then snuggled her closer and let the lassitude take him. And he smiled when he felt her turn her head and gently kiss the side of his shoulder.

Later—much later, he realized when he glanced at the clock—he roused from a deep, dreamless sleep. Dreamless. It occurred to him suddenly that he hadn't had the dream since he'd met Sydney. It wasn't all that remarkable, considering the infrequency with which it attacked these days, but still… Any change in his routine usually brought on bouts of vivid, horrifying dreams in which he was about to be kidnapped. And this was definitely a change in his routine.

He tightened his arms around Sydney. Man. If he weren't still holding her in his arms, he'd have sworn he'd just had the most erotic dream of his entire life. He'd been attracted to her since the first day he'd seen her, had known she could get him hard faster than anything he'd ever experienced before. He'd known, on some primitive level that he couldn't explain, that sex with her would be fantastic.

But he'd never expected that behind her calm, capable facade, she was a screaming wildcat who would blow the top of his head off. He smiled in the darkness. What a woman.

She had turned onto her side and was snuggled spoon-fashion in front of him, her soft bottom nestled against his thighs. He enjoyed the closeness. Felicia had been one of those sleepers who threw arms and legs every which way and there'd been plenty of space between them in their king-size bed most of the time.

Felicia. Thinking of his wife brought all the craziness of the recent days back to the forefront of his mind, and suddenly he was wide awake. What was he doing? What the hell was he doing? Sydney had said she loved him.

And he'd wanted desperately just to open his mouth and say it back. But he couldn't. One of them had to be sensible. This wasn't real. This was…pretend. Once they got the details of Nick's new life straightened out and he was home again with his son, she'd feel differently.

Dawn was just pearling the sky outside when he woke again. Sydney was still curled in his arms just as she'd been all night. After several hours of sleep, his body was letting him know it would be happy to indulge in some early-morning lovemaking, but he resisted the urge to lift Sydney's thigh over his and slide into her while she was still warm and sleepy.

Instead, he carefully got out from beneath the covers. He took his clothes and went through the apartment to the half bath off the kitchen so he didn't wake Sydney. He splashed water on his face and shoved back his hair, then dressed rapidly. His brain was moving twice as fast, though, and he couldn't stop thinking about what was happening.

He knew what Sydney wanted. Even if she hadn't said it, hadn't even allowed herself to think it, he knew. He stepped out of the bathroom and went to the kitchen, where he'd left his keys on the counter last night.

But as he turned to go, Sydney appeared in the hallway that led from the bedrooms. Her hair was messy, her eyes heavy-lidded and sexy. She'd thrown on an aqua robe in some satiny material, and he could see the tight tips of her breasts pressing against the fabric. The robe was short, tempting him to go to her and slip his hand beneath its bottom edge, to find the sweet, hot center of her and assuage the raging need that still hadn't subsided fully.

"What are you doing?" she asked, yawning. But she'd seen the keys in his hand, and the sleepiness had fled from her eyes, leaving them wary and slightly puzzled.

"I have to go."

"No, you don't." She started toward him. "You can stay and have breakfast with us."

"I have to go," he repeated. It would be all too easy to let himself slide into a relationship with her, but that was the one thing he couldn't do.

"All right," Sydney said quietly, raising one eyebrow. He could almost hear what she was thinking. *Uh-oh. He's touchy this morning.* "Shall I get Nick's usual baby-sitter today?"

"No, I'll be back. How long do you think it will be until I can take him home?"

She went very still. "You mean back to the island."

"Yes."

"I don't know." She spread her hands. "You heard what the counselor said. But, Danny, have you really thought about how difficult that's going to be for Nick? And for you as well? Wouldn't it be better if you moved back to Portland? You'd have your family's support and Nick could grow up with an extended family that he's rarely going to see if you take him away."

"No," he said through his teeth. "It would *not* be better. I'm perfectly happy on the island."

"But will Nick be?"

"I'm taking him home with me," he said forcefully. "Soon."

Sydney threw her hands in the air. "Why won't you think about how difficult this is going to be for him?" She pointed an accusing finger at him. "You don't love that island for what it is, Danny. You told me it was a hideout, remember? Well, you can't keep hiding from the world. You have this whole mountain of guilt that you wallow in, and you think if you keep yourself wrapped in bland, meaningless days, you can avoid it."

"That's not true!" He welcomed the anger that rushed through him, concentrating on it to get him through this and out the door.

"It is true," she challenged. "You can't forgive yourself for the past—for letting Robbie down, for letting Nick get taken, too. You even think you should have kept Felicia from killing herself. I don't think you even realize how guilty you feel, and how it's poisoning your chance at a good life. A normal life. Your attitude could be bad for a little boy. You could change Nick from the person he is to someone who's a far less happy adult. Is that what you want?"

"You don't know anything about me or my life!" he shot back. "How could you possibly understand?"

"I do have some idea of what you've been through. But you can't let it keep running your life."

He narrowed his eyes, too furious to censor his words, to think about what he was saying. "Do you think I don't know what your motive is here, Sydney? It's obvious you're angling for a way to keep Nick in your life. And if you try to keep him away from me, that makes you as bad as the people who took him in the first place."

She froze, all color draining from her face.

Too late, he realized how out of line that accusation had been. "I'm sorry," he said wearily. "I appreciate everything you've done for Nick. I do. I'd like to remunerate you in some way for all the years—"

She quivered as if he'd struck her. "Pay me?" she whispered. "You want to pay me for loving him?"

There was a look on her face he'd never seen there before, as if someone had just told her Nick had died or something.

"Leave," she said in that same too-quiet tone. "Leave now. Let me know when you've made arrangements to take Nick away, but don't come back here. Ever. I'll tell him you're his father."

And before he could think of anything to say, she turned and walked back to her bedroom, closing the door behind her.

"Sydney!" Panic began to curl around the edges of his rage. He followed her but when he put his hand on the knob, the bedroom door had been locked. He considered breaking it down for about one second, but that would wake Nick, and the last thing he wanted was for his son to see them fighting.

Slowly he turned and made his way from her apartment, shell-shocked by the way things had blown up in his face.

She'd had no right to say all those things, he told himself as he slid behind the wheel of his rental car. But…hadn't she? If it weren't for her, his son might not even be alive today. If it weren't for her bone-deep honesty, he wouldn't even know Nick was still alive.

He gripped the steering wheel so tightly his fingers ached. What had he done? What the hell had he done?

And more importantly, why?

# *Thirteen*

*I never should have said yes.* Everett paced the floor inside Nancy's cozy apartment. For once he didn't even see the pretty rose and green accents, the plants she tended so lovingly, the special little touches that made her place a home instead of just a place to live. Every two seconds he checked the clock again.

"Everett," said Nancy. "Come sit down. They'll be here any minute."

"That's what I'm afraid of," he muttered, and she chuckled. "Relax. Your parents can't wait to meet you. But they don't want to rush you. When they called and I suggested you meet here, they were very concerned about whether or not you were ready to talk to them, remember?"

He remembered. But it didn't help much. Any second now, the two people who'd given him life were going to walk through that door. He felt doubly guilty for wanting to bolt. Many adopted kids would give a limb to know their birth parents. His situation wasn't that much different. Except that most kids hadn't deliberately helped someone try to ruin their parents' life's work.

The doorbell rang, and he felt as if he had leaped a foot in the air.

Nancy rose. "Let me get it." She paused as she reached him, stretching up to kiss his chin. "It's going to be okay."

He stayed where he was by the window when she welcomed the couple in. As they moved into his line of sight, he felt a shock wave roll through him. The man—his father—had silver hair at his temples and more wrinkles, but the face that looked at him was shockingly similar to the face he saw in the mirror every day.

Mrs. Logan was tall, even taller than Nancy, whom he knew was five-foot-nine. Her hair still retained reddish-gold highlights. Her brown eyes were filled with tears.

They didn't crowd him. He had to give them credit. The woman, in particular, fairly vibrated with the need to rush forward and hug him, but she contented herself with giving Nancy a warm embrace.

"Thank you, dear, for offering to host us this afternoon."

"You're most welcome. Please, have a seat. Can I get either of you something to drink?"

Terrence and Leslie Logan both shook their heads as they sank onto the loveseat Nancy indicated. "No, thank you," said Terrence. He smiled slightly. "We're so nervous we'd probably spill it all over your rugs."

Nancy smiled calmly. "Everett's been a nervous wreck, too." She took a seat on the couch opposite the couple and patted the cushion beside her. "Quit hovering over there, Everett."

Reluctantly, he left the relative security of his isolated spot at the window. As he sat down beside Nancy, she slipped her hand into his. Immediately, he felt better, just as he had at the police station. He took a deep breath. "Hello," he said, extending a hand over the coffee table that separated him from his father and mother. "I'm Everett now, but I was—am—your son Robbie."

Tears rolled down Leslie's face as Terrence reached out and gave his hand a firm shake. "Sorry," she managed.

"It's all right," Nancy said. She reached for a box of tissues she'd placed nearby. "I'm prepared."

Leslie laughed. "Wise woman." She took a tissue from the box Nancy extended and wiped her eyes. "This is just so overwhelming," she said.

Nancy took a tissue and dabbed at her own eyes before she set down the box. "You wouldn't be human if you weren't emotionally shaken by seeing your son for the first time in almost three decades."

"We thought you were dead," Leslie said to her son. "For years and years. And all the time you were out there somewhere." Her voice broke again. "We're so sorry. If we'd known, we *never* would have stopped looking for you."

*They* were sorry? "You have nothing to apologize for," he said, meaning it.

Terrence cleared his throat and Everett saw that his eyes were a bit shiny as well. What was wrong with him, that he didn't feel like crying? All he felt like doing was running and hiding in a hole somewhere.

"No one has any apologies to make," said the man who'd fathered him. The natural air of authority that surrounded him told Everett that people rarely argued with Terrence Logan.

Everett tried a smile. He didn't know what to say, so he said nothing.

"The police tell us they've agreed not to prosecute you since you were so helpful to them," Leslie said. He was surprised that she was willing to bring up the most painful issue between them, but he was glad as well. Might as well get it out right away, let them know he understood that they probably didn't want much to do with him after what he'd done. Nancy had told him again and again that his family had forgiven him, that they couldn't wait to meet him. But he couldn't figure out why. He was nothing special.

"Did you know they've located three of the missing children already?" Leslie continued.

Everett shifted uncomfortably. "Good." His voice sounded rusty.

There was an awkward silence.

"So," said Nancy, "tell us about your family. Everett knows he has brothers and sisters, but not many details."

Leslie Logan's face brightened. She seized on the subject gratefully and within minutes, Nancy had the conversation rolling easily along. Everett could have kissed her. Correction. Once the Logans were gone, he *would* kiss her. Every sweet inch of her. She had stuck by his side when many women would have been long gone. Did she have any idea how much he loved her?

Probably not. He'd never been very good with words, so he'd never thought to offer them. *I love you.* He practiced the words in his head. He could say them. He didn't trust his judgment about many things, but Nancy Allen had all but written her feelings for him on a billboard. He was nearly certain she loved him. If not, she had done a mighty good job of faking it. And he was pretty sure she wasn't faking.

In any case, Nancy had taken enough of the risks in their relationship. Tonight he would tell her he loved her.

He shifted his attention back to the Logans. They were…interesting. They finished each other's sentences, touched each other lightly, occasionally exchanged a glance or a smile that clearly was a private communication just between the two of them. He figured they'd been married now for around forty years.

That was one long marriage. What could make people stay together for that long?

His gaze strayed to Nancy again, gesturing with her hands as she spoke with Leslie. And he knew. Love. Love was what kept couples together for decades. A bone-deep certainty that this was the person you wanted to be with every day for the rest of your life.

The way he felt about Nancy.

Suddenly he knew what he was going to do tonight. He didn't have the money for an engagement ring, but he was going to ask Nancy to marry him. If she was the woman he thought she was, she wouldn't care about a ring or lack of one.

He felt something inside him subtly shift and relax once he'd made the decision. His beautiful, compassionate, strong nurse had been meant for him. It was time he showed her that he knew it.

Somehow, an hour had passed. The dreaded visit hadn't been nearly the ordeal he'd anticipated, largely thanks to Nancy.

Terrence Logan had risen to escort his wife to the door. It was impossible for Everett to think of the couple as his parents. He felt little connection to them despite their obvious happiness at having found him. But something had been bothering him.

"Mr. Logan?"

Terrence and Leslie both stopped and turned. "Yes?" said Terrence.

"I have to— I mean, I wanted to ask you something." Everett stopped nervously and waited.

Terrence smiled. "I'll do my best to find an answer. What is it?"

"When I was little—before I was taken, I mean—did we ever go to a major league baseball game?"

Leslie Logan said, "Oh!" and pressed the fingers of both hands hard against her lips. Her husband's face lit up as if he were a child seeing Santa for the first time.

"Yes," he said. "When you were five, we took you up to Seattle for a few days. You and I went to see the Mariners play the Toronto Blue Jays in the Kingdome. That was a long time ago, before they tore it down and built the new stadium. It was your very first pro game and you were so excited you could barely sit still."

"I remember," said Everett. Wonder and pleasure washed through him as if he were that little boy again. "I remember! You bought me a Mariners pennant and we hung it over my bed when we got home."

"Yes." Terrence's eyes filled with tears. "I still have that pennant in a box of things we saved from your room when we moved from the house in Spring Heights." He hesitated. "Sometime perhaps you'd like to see the stuff we kept, like your rock collection."

Leslie gave a quavering laugh. "That's a generous term for it," she told Everett. "You picked up every hunk of gravel we passed when you were small. Your pockets got so loaded down with rocks you were in danger of losing your pants."

"We have a great picture of you holding up your shorts with both hands," Terrence said. "You were about three, I believe."

Nancy was laughing lightly. "I'd love to see that sometime."

"We'd love to show it to you. Both of you." Leslie took a deep breath. As if she couldn't help herself, she reached out and patted Everett's forearm gently. "We don't want to rush you, Everett. Finding that you have a family as big as ours must be daunting. But if you two would like to come to dinner some evening, perhaps the four of us could look at some of those old photos together. Or just sit and visit a little more."

Terrence nodded. "Your brothers and sisters are dying to meet you, but we convinced them it would be premature to mob you. And maybe we're a little selfish. We'd like to have you to ourselves for a while before we have to share you."

Goosebumps ran up his spine as the affection in his father's and mother's voices penetrated. He'd been loved. *He still was loved.* A year ago his life had been dreary and empty, filled only with erroneous information and Charlie's false words.

Now, despite everything that had occurred, he felt a cautious bud of happiness unfurling in his heart. These people had loved him when he was a child, as much as any child could ever wish to be loved. The empty spaces inside him were empty no longer, filled by Nancy and now by these wonderful, generous parents he was just beginning to know.

He cleared his throat. "I'd like to see those photographs with you," he told them. "I'd like to remember more about my life with you. I'd even like to meet your—the rest of my family."

Nancy laughed, and he noticed there were tears in her eyes now, too. "Coming from Everett, that's nothing less than a miracle. Groups of people aren't usually his thing."

He smiled. A real smile that felt natural. "She knows me too well. One or two at a time might be nice."

Terrence chuckled. "Don't blame you a bit."

Leslie was searching his face. "I shouldn't ask this, but…would you mind if I hugged you?"

His insides turned to a quivering mass of jelly. "Uh, no. I guess not."

She had her arms around him almost before he'd finished the words. It felt weird and strange—and *wonderful*. Hesitantly, he lifted his own hands and patted her back as she sobbed against his shoulder. After a moment, he let himself hug her, a little shocked by how much he'd needed this. Then his father moved in to share the embrace, and he had to close his eyes against a strong wave of emotion. He'd longed for a real, loving family as a lonely little boy, and now he'd been handed one, despite all the trouble he'd helped cause. It was a miracle.

He looked over his mother's head at his own personal miracle, and Nancy blew him a kiss.

He smiled. And blew one back.

"Nick?" Sydney forced herself to dredge up a light tone later that morning. After she was sure Danny had left her apartment earlier, she'd called in sick just before 8:00 a.m. Sooner or later she was going to have to start thinking about work again, but right now it was beyond her.

Pain burned, a searing inferno that incinerated her heart. He was right, and she couldn't deny it. She had been dreaming of a life with him, even if she'd never let herself say it, or even think it. Even though he'd told her over and over that he didn't have feelings for her, at least none that he was willing to admit to, she'd been so sure of the extraordinary bond growing between them that her heart had kept hope alive.

She couldn't have been more wrong. Danny was returning to Hawaii. With Nick. Without her. A sob bubbled up and nearly escaped before she caught it. She meant nothing to him. Nothing more than a woman to whom he'd always be grateful for taking care of his son.

Grateful enough to offer her money. That thought brought a surge of anger flooding back. If he was that stupid, then she didn't want him anyway.

*Right, Sydney. If you say it often enough, maybe someday you'll even believe it.*

Her son looked up from the book of mazes he was diligently working his way through when she called his name. "Uh-huh?"

"I need to talk to you for a sec. Can you come here?"

Obediently, the little boy laid down his crayon and skipped across the floor, skidding into her lap in a dive when he was close enough.

Sydney caught him, pulling him close and kissing his neck until he screamed for mercy. Then he said, "Whatcha wanna talk about, Mommy?"

*Dear God, help me find the right words.* She took a deep breath. "Honey, do you remember when I told you your other mommy left you with me before she died?"

"Uh-huh."

"Well, I just found out not long ago that I was wrong about that."

He turned puzzled blue eyes up to her. "How come?"

"The lady who left you with me wasn't your mommy, after all. She was not a very nice person, and she helped take you from your real mommy and daddy who loved you very much."

Nick's eyes were enormous. "I had a daddy, too?"

The innocent question, straight to the heart of the matter in typical Nick-fashion, cut deep. Many times she'd worried about whether the lack of a man in her life would affect her son. She nodded. "You had a daddy, too." Then she stopped again, marshalling her thoughts.

But Nick clearly was thinking thoughts of his own. "Was I kidcatched?"

"Kidnapped," she corrected gently, though her son's creative word was actually closer to the truth. "Yes. When you were just one year old, bad people stole you."

"What happened to that mommy and daddy?" he asked. "I bet they cried."

"Oh, they did," she assured him, her throat aching with the effort it took to force out the words in a normal tone. "They loved you very much and they were terribly sad when you were taken away. They called the police and everybody looked and looked, but no one ever found you."

"You found me," he pointed out.

"Yes, but I didn't know who you were." She ran a hand through his silky blond hair. "I just knew you were the most wonderful little boy in the world and I wanted to be your mommy."

"And you are!"

If she weren't working so hard not to break down, she might have laughed at his wondering tone. With a five-year-old's lack of comprehension, he apparently thought that because she wanted him, he was brought to her—rather than the other way around. He didn't fully realize that having a twelve-month-old infant dumped in her lap might not be every woman's idea of a miracle. Lucky for him, it had been hers.

She didn't say anything else, mindful of the therapist's advice to take it at Nick's pace. When he had digested the information and was ready to talk, she would tell him more.

But she'd forgotten the astute brain in that little head. He often surprised her with his intellect; why should today be any different?

"Hey, Mommy?"

"Mm-hmm?"

"What happened to my other mommy? Not the one who died. The other one. And the daddy?"

She realized Nick was a little confused about Margo, but since he'd gotten the gist of the explanation, she could save clarity for another time. Or Danny could, she amended, feeling the pain that was so rapidly becoming familiar fill her heart. "Well, I told you they missed you, right? The mommy was very, very sad, and after a little while she died."

"What about the daddy? Did he die, too?" Death was an abstract concept to Nick, who'd never even seen a pet pass away, much less someone he loved. His tone was calm and interested.

"No," she said. "The daddy didn't die. He's still alive and he knows you are, too, and he's very happy."

"I have a daddy?" This was big news. She'd bet he was already imagining telling his little pal Zachary.

"You do."

He considered this for a moment. "That's okay," he decided finally. "I don't need more mommies 'cuz I already have you. But a daddy would be fun." He looked at her again, suddenly vulnerable. "Right?"

"Right," she said firmly. "Very fun. In fact, you've already been having fun with your daddy, only you didn't know he was your daddy." She hadn't really planned on going quite this far today, but since Nick seemed to be dealing with it so well, she might as well keep talking.

"Who is he? It can't be Uncle Stu because he's got Aunt Patti and she's still alive."

"Right. It's someone who's been playing with you a lot lately, someone who's been spending a lot of time—"

"Danny!" Nick all but shouted the name as she nodded. "Danny's my daddy!" He jumped from her lap and bounced up and down as if his legs were made of springs. "Oh-boy-oh-boy-oh-boy! Danny's fun," he informed her, as if that were the most important criterion for the role of father. Then he stopped bouncing. "When's he coming over?"

"I don't know." Though it was the last thing she wanted to do, she rose and headed for the telephone. "I guess I'd better call and ask him."

While he was in the shower, Sydney had called to tell him she'd told Nick about his parentage. She'd left only a brief and impersonal message. He had no idea how Nick had taken the news.

Danny stood by the phone in his hotel room, wondering what his son was doing. What Sydney was doing. Were they crying together? Was Nick devastated at the thought of leaving his home?

*Of course he is, you idiot. What kid wants to leave everything familiar and go away with some guy he's known a few days?*

His mind immediately made the leap to Robbie Logan, torn from his family at nearly the same tender age Nick was now. It had scarred him deeply, if his involvement in the kidnapping ring was any indication. But it had scarred Danny as well. Sydney was right, he acknowledged. He had been avoiding life. And it was time he stopped.

He reached for the phone book. He had no idea how to contact Robbie—Everett now—but the Logans probably would. For years he'd assumed they hated him. Assumed they blamed him for the kidnapping.

Now, thinking of Nick, he realized how very young he'd been. Maybe Leslie Logan hadn't been angry at him that day.

He held his finger beneath the Logans' number as he punched the buttons of the phone.

Two short hours later, he parked in front of a shabby apartment building. Consulting the address Leslie had given him, he found the proper door, knocked and waited.

The door opened so fast that the man inside must have been standing there waiting. He didn't speak for a moment, only stood there staring back at Danny.

He looks like his father. That was Danny's first thought. Tall and good-looking, although this man didn't project the air of self-confidence that was so much a part of Terrence Logan.

Everett Baker seemed apprehensive and Danny could practically see what it took him to make the social effort. Finally, he said, "You haven't changed."

Danny almost smiled. "Your mother said the same thing."

"I was sorry to hear about your son," Everett said. Danny gauged his face, seeing nothing but sincerity. Still… "Before we go one step further, I have to ask you— Did you have anything to do with Noah's kidnapping?"

Everett stood silent for a moment, then said, "I don't blame you for asking." Then he shook his head. "No. But I suspect one of the men I was involved with might have. I've already given the police all the information I have."

Danny gauged Everett's expression. He appeared to be telling the truth. "Thank you," he said more quietly. "I had to know."

"Everett?" A slender, pretty woman with brown hair stood behind him. "Are you going to invite him in?" Her voice was light and teasing, and Danny was astonished by the expression of tenderness that passed over his childhood friend's face.

Everett opened the door wider. "Please come in," he said. "I'd like to introduce you to my fiancée, Nancy Allen."

Much later, sitting in his solitary hotel room, Danny was still thinking about Everett Baker. His childhood friend was clearly changed by his kidnapping experience. Probably the only thing that had saved him was Nancy Allen, the woman he was going to marry. According to Everett, she'd believed in him long before he believed in himself. It warmed a tiny part of Danny's heart to see that his old friend might finally find the happiness and love that must have been denied him for most of his life.

The telephone rang and he lifted the receiver. "Hello?"

"Are you coming to work today or not?" It was Trent, sounding as if he were trying to be belligerent, but failing.

"Don't think so," said Danny.

"What's wrong?" Trent was instantly suspicious.

Danny sighed. "I visited Everett Baker today."

"You're kidding!"

"And now I'm looking at my own life and not liking some of the things I'm seeing."

"Such as?"

"I'm going to ask you a straight question. Answer it straight or I'll come over there and kick your ass."

"At least that would be one way to get you into the office again."

Danny smiled. Then he said, "Have I been wallowing in my own problems for too long?"

There was a long silence. "Who told you that?"

"Never mind. The answer is yes, isn't it?"

Trent exhaled heavily. "Hell, Danny, I don't know. Very few people would be qualified to tell you you're overdoing the grief thing. Look at what you've gone through in your life."

"I know. But I think I might have had a chance to change that, and I blew it." That was true. After this morning Sydney would never speak to him again, he was certain. Except for things pertaining to Nick.

"Ah, damn. Did you say something dumb to Sydney?"

"Why would you think that?"

"You're a guy," Trent said dryly. "Ask Peter, or

Ivy's king, or any man you know. We have a distinct tendency to insert our feet into our mouths frequently. Shoes and all."

"These were boots. Snowshoes. Skis, even."

"Go get 'em out," Trent said promptly. "Sydney is the best thing that's ever happened to you—and not just because she saved your son and was big-hearted enough to return him to you."

*Sydney is the best thing that's ever happened to you.* It was true. And he'd ruined it. He winced as he recalled the harsh words he'd thrown at her just after dawn. True happiness was a valuable thing. Trent and his sisters had found it, so had Everett. And so had he. Only he probably had demolished it when he'd hurt Sydney.

Was it possible there could be a life with her? Did he dare let himself believe it?

The answer was like a shotgun fired right beside his ear. Of course! He hadn't dared to let himself believe that his son was still living, and look how wrong he'd been about that. Now he had Nick back, but he would only be living half a life if Sydney wasn't a daily part of it. And not for Nick's sake.

She'd saved him.

He thought of the shattered hurt in her blue eyes and realized he might not get another chance. But he wasn't going to slink away without trying this time.

Picking up the phone book for the second time that day, he rapidly flipped through the pages. If he was going to try to get Sydney to forgive him, he had a lot to do today.

## *Fourteen*

The doorbell rang just before five o'clock. Sydney took a deep, bracing breath. *You can do this,* she lectured herself. *You can.*

"Danny!" Nick shouted. He leaped to his feet and began to race across the room. At the door, he paused and looked back at her. "May I open it?"

She nodded. Took another deep breath.

Nick yanked the door open.

"Hey, buddy," Danny said. "How are you?"

Nick didn't answer. He stood very still, looking up at the big man. Sydney could only see him from the back. He looked very little and very vulnerable.

Danny crouched. "So you and your mommy had a talk, huh?"

Nick nodded, a hint of that vulnerability in his tone as he said, "Are you really my daddy?"

Danny took a deep breath. "Yeah. I really am."

Nick tipped his head to one side. "An' you didn't want to let me get kidcatched?"

"No." It sounded as if Danny nearly choked on the word but he forced a few more out. "I wish it had never happened."

Nick thought some more. "Good," he said. He reached out and took Danny's hand. "I have a new project for my next boys' club project. Will you help me? Daddies do that stuff, you know."

Danny managed a smile. "Sure. I'll see what I can do." As his son's small hand slipped into his, he looked across the room at Sydney, smiling. She looked away.

"I have a surprise for your mommy," he said to Nick. "But we have to take her for a ride to see it."

Dammit! That wasn't fair, and if Nick weren't standing there she'd have let him have it. Then she realized he'd done it *because* Nick was there. He knew that she wouldn't refuse in front of the child.

"Come on, Mommy!" Nick shouted. "You got a surprise! Let's go see it."

She rose from the couch and retrieved her purse from the closet. "All right." She trailed behind the two males, locking the door and pulling it closed. But when she got to Danny's car, he was holding her door open and Nick was already in the back, in a brand-new car seat.

She couldn't look at him. It just hurt too much, so

she scooted into the passenger seat with her head down. Danny went around to the driver's side.

It was a quiet trip, broken only by Nick's chatter as he made wild, ridiculous guesses about what the surprise could be. After twenty minutes, Danny pulled into a driveway with a gate across it. He lifted a small device and punched a button and the gate slid open. "Cool, huh?" he said over his shoulder.

"Cool," Nick agreed. "Where we goin'?"

"Just up here."

She was puzzled. Whom was he taking them to visit and why would he be opening their gate?

They drove along a short driveway around a curve. Trees grew closely on both sides of the driveway, but as they rounded the curve, the view opened up onto a spacious green lawn. Ahead of them was a stunningly beautiful house built of gray stone with lots of windows sparkling in the late-day light. It was a rancher on a small rise, but the hill fell away to the right and as they drove around and parked, she could see that there was a second story below the main level that opened onto an exquisite terrace with a swimming pool nearby.

"A pool!"

"Cool," Danny finished dryly. "Let's go inside."

"Who lives here?"

Sydney blessed her son. She hadn't had to ask a single question.

Danny didn't answer. Leaving Sydney to get out of the car and unbuckle Nick, he walked ahead to the double front door and inserted a key from his pocket. Then he stood aside as Nick came flying up the walk. "Go on in," he said.

Sydney walked past, doing her best not to brush against him. Then she stopped. The house was empty. Empty?

She turned to Danny, bracing herself to meet his eyes. "What's going on?" For once, Nick seemed speechless.

"I bought a house this afternoon," he told her. His eyes were warm and there was no trace of the anger he'd spat at her earlier.

"Congratulations," she said formally. She'd made the mistake before of thinking that look in his eyes meant something special, and she'd been wrong. She wouldn't fall for it again. Then she realized what the house meant. "You're staying in Portland? At least part-time?"

He nodded, smiling. "At least part-time. It depends on some other things."

*Like what?* But she didn't say it aloud.

His smile fell. "Aren't you going to ask me about those other things?"

She shrugged. "It's none of my business."

"I think maybe it is," he said. Then he turned to Nick. "Let's take Mommy out back."

They walked through the house. It was utterly, utterly lovely. The kitchen was spacious and light, and Danny led them to French doors at its other end. "Out here," he said.

Nick darted past him out the door. A second later she heard her son squeal, "Oh, boy! Ohboyohboyohboy!"

"Wha—?" She stepped onto the terrace. Danny's brother Trent stood at one side. Dancing around him on a leash was a puppy. A *huge* puppy. Black and fuzzy, and currently licking her son's face as he knelt on the ground beside it.

"Oh," she said. "He's wanted a dog for so long. And this will be a perfect place to raise it."

"I thought he might be a bear cub when I first saw him," he said. "He's a Newfoundland puppy. Ten weeks old."

"Just a baby," she murmured.

"But I'm not sure I can keep it," Danny said.

"What? Then you shouldn't have let him see it," she began sharply. Then the smile on his face registered. Her heart stuttered but she told herself to ignore it. That smile wasn't for her. "What's going on?" she asked again, suspiciously. She just wanted to go home. Being this close to him was breaking her heart into even smaller pieces than it already was.

"The dog needs a family," he told her. "Not just a lonely man and a little boy." He took a deep breath. "Last night you told me you loved me. This morning I said some pretty unforgivable things. But, Sydney, I'm asking—*begging*—you to forgive me, anyway."

She was stunned. Rooted to the spot. She felt tears sting her eyes.

"I'm a coward," Danny told her. "It was a lot easier to hide than to risk rejection. You were right about me being angry at Felicia. But what I also realized is I've given my past too much power over the rest of my life. I'm not going to let myself be afraid to take risks anymore. I promised myself that this morning."

Sydney didn't know what to say. She wanted to throw her arms around him and tell him he wasn't a coward, that he was the bravest man she knew. But he hadn't said any of the words she most needed to hear, and she was the coward now, afraid to misinterpret his meaning.

Danny dug into his pants pocket. He withdrew a tiny jeweler's box, dropping onto one knee before her as he did so. "Sydney," he said, "I love you. I dream of you all the time. Will you marry me? Not," he rushed on, "just so we can give Nick a family, but because you love me, too."

She opened her mouth, then closed it again as she sank to her knees beside him. In his eyes, she saw the confidence and love she'd longed for. He'd found himself, she realized, and come to terms with his past.

And finally he could look at the future.

He flipped up the lid of the box to show her a striking, sparkling blue sapphire set amid several smaller diamonds. "It matches your eyes," he said.

She took a deep breath. "I have loved you," she said, "since the first time you kissed me on your island. Before I ever knew you were Nick's father. There's nothing I want more than to spend the rest of my life with you."

Danny smiled. He took the ring from the box and slid it onto her finger, then drew her to him and kissed her with all the passion he'd shown her in the past. "Will you live here in this house with me?"

"You and a young boy and a puppy?" she asked, laughing. "I'd love to."

"There are several extra bedrooms," he informed her.

"Danny!" She pretended shock. "Not in front of your son and your brother."

He raised his eyebrows, laughing out loud. Somewhere along the way, she realized, Danny's laughter had returned. His smiles had grown from bare curls at the corners of his mouth to the beautiful, flashing grin she saw every day on the face of their son. "I meant for more children," he said. "But if you want to test-drive all of them first, I guess I'm up for that."

Now it was her turn to laugh.

Across the terrace, Nick turned and hollered, "Hey! Trent says he's my uncle now! Can I have this dog, Mommy? He can sleep on my bed and I'll feed him and everything!"

# Epilogue

*Five months later...*

It was the biggest holiday party Sydney had ever imagined, and the most unusual. Almost all the members of the Logan and Crosby families had accepted Danny's and Sydney's invitation to join them on Nanilani for a post Christmas gathering. Though they lived at the big house in Portland now, Danny had told Sydney that they would always keep the island where they'd met.

On the fourth day of the week-long vacation, Sydney opened the doors that led onto the lanai for Leilani. In the housekeeper's hands was an extraordinary cake, decorated with a family crest.

"Hey, everybody, look at this thing!" called Sydney's sister-in-law Ivy as Leilani set the cake on the long table at one side of the terrace already loaded with traditional Christmas dishes.

"Is that the new design?" asked Ivy's husband, Max von Husden. Max peered down at the cake as he juggled their eight-month-old son in his arms. Funny, thought Sydney, to imagine that baby was a prince who would take his father's place on the throne of Lantanya one day.

"It is," Katie Logan said in answer to Max's question. "What do you think?"

"I think it's beautiful," pronounced Ivy. "A crest that unites the emblems of the Crosby and Logan families was a perfect idea for your family."

"Have you seen the ring?" Leslie Logan asked. Every inch the proud grandmother, she held a wriggling infant boy in her arms. "It's on that table over there, in the white box."

The ring Leslie referred to was a birth ring she'd had designed for Katie and her husband Peter's first child. Today's party had been an excuse to unite both families as well as to visit with everyone Danny and Sydney hadn't seen in the months since they'd been married. The only family member not invited was Danny's mother Sheila, who had forfeited any right to be part of the family with her hateful, manipulative actions. Sydney had met the woman once, storming out of Trent's office after some tantrum, and once had definitely been enough.

Sydney looked across the lanai. Standing by the railing that looked out toward Kauai, Danny, his brother Trent, their half brother, Jackson, and father, Jack, stood talking casually. Her heart swelled with love when her husband caught her eye and smiled. "You all right?" he mouthed.

She nodded. Just then, Nick and his younger cousin Tyler, Jackson's son, barreled into the middle of the crowd. Barking loudly behind them came Wildman, Nick's dog. The Newfoundland pup easily outweighed at least half the wedding guests, she thought wryly, and he wasn't even a year old yet.

"Whoa there, fellas!" Jackson's wife, Laurel, adroitly caught each boy around the waist as they ran past her. "This isn't the place to be ripping around. Why don't you two go out on the lawn? And take him with you," she said, pointing sternly to the big dog.

Jack Crosby's second wife, Toni, joined the group. Sydney would always have a soft spot for Toni ever since she'd learned that Toni had been instrumental in helping Trent convince Jack to get Danny out of that horrible school so many years ago. "Any chance I could hold that baby?" Toni said wistfully to Leslie.

"Of course." Leslie grinned. She handed Kate and Peter's son to Toni. "There are plenty more around here to snuggle. She beckoned to her son David's wife, Elizabeth. Their adopted daughter Natasha slept soundly on her mother's shoulder while David and his twin sister Jillian stood nearby, heads close together as they conversed. "I'll take her," Leslie announced, smiling warmly at her daughter-in-law.

Moving through the group, Sydney stopped to exchange a word with FBI agents Sam Jones and his wife Bridget Logan-Jones, and Bridget's brother Eric and his wife, Jenny. Sydney noticed Jenny kept an eagle eye on their son, Cole, while still participating in the conversation.

"...and Morgan is fairly pleased with the way Children's Connection has weathered the scandal," Bridget was saying. Morgan Davis was the director of the organization and had worked hard to get them positive publicity in the wake of Charlie Prescott's damaging deeds.

"How's it going with Reya?" Sydney asked. Morgan and his wife, Emma, had recently adopted their first child, a girl, through Children's Connection.

"Emma says she's an angel," Jenny reported, smiling. Her warm blue eyes looked at Sydney critically. "You should be resting."

Sydney smiled. "I'd love a nap," she said, "but not just yet."

Trent's wife, Rebecca, was seated at one of the cocktail tables and Sydney walked in that direction.

"Sit down and take a load off," Rebecca said to Sydney.

"Thanks." Sydney eased into a chair. Her feet were screaming for relief.

"You know," said Rebecca, "you're *enormous* for barely six months along."

"Thanks so much," said Sydney. "Actually, there's a reason for my size."

Rebecca's eyebrows rose. "Oh?" Then her face lit up. "Oh! Don't tell me you're going to have twins!"

"Okay, I won't," Sydney said.

Rebecca squealed. "Oh, Sydney, this is so exciting!"

Trent had come over and placed his hands on his wife's shoulders. "Danny just told us the news," he said to Sydney. "Congratulations."

She nodded. "Thank you."

"We, uh, have a little news of our own," he went on.

Sydney's gaze darted to Rebecca's face. She was looking up at her husband with a look of such love that Sydney felt her throat close up. "Oh, Rebecca," she said. "When?"

"In about seven months," her friend said. "We just found out."

"That's wonderful!" Sydney was close to tears. She'd say a prayer every day that this pregnancy went well.

Just then a movement near the door caught her attention. Danny's father, Terrence, entered the room. At his side were another couple and as she recognized them, Sydney heaved herself to her feet. "They came! I wasn't sure they would."

With Terrence was his son Everett, and Everett's brand-new wife, Nancy. Danny had seen them, too, and he was moving forward from the opposite side of the lanai.

They reached the new arrivals at the same time.

"Merry Christmas. We're so pleased you could come," Sydney said.

"We're delighted to be here," Nancy said, kissing her cheek. "Leslie told me that this is the last trip your doctor's letting you take. How are you feeling?"

Sydney waved her hand. "Better some days than others. It'll be nice to be able to see my feet again."

Nancy chuckled. At the same time she reached back and casually drew Everett forward from where he'd been hovering behind her.

"Hello," he said formally.

"Welcome to Hawaii," Sydney said. None of them had been confident that Everett would feel comfortable enough to join the combined Crosby-Logan family gathering, or if the terms of his probation would even permit him to travel out-of-state.

"Glad you could make it," Danny added.

Everett looked at him solemnly. "Thank you for inviting us."

Danny nodded. "You'd better come over here and say hello to your mother. Looks like she's dying to smother you with kisses again."

Everett looked so dismayed that everyone laughed, but he dutifully accompanied Nancy across the terrace as Terrence followed the couple.

"I'll go rescue him in a few minutes and find him

a quiet corner," Danny said. "He'll be happier if he's not the center of attention."

Sydney slid her arm around his lean waist as she surveyed the crowd. "Could you ever have imagined this a year ago?" she asked.

Danny pulled her against him, careful to angle her so her belly didn't get squashed. "No," he said in a husky voice. "A year ago, I was just trying to get through one day at a time." He smoothed his hand over her cheek and tipped her face up to his. "The day you washed up on my beach was the best day of my life."

"I'm not sure it was the best day of mine," she said wryly, remembering the lump on her head, "but since it resulted in this," she said, indicating the group on the terrace as well as the two of them, "I guess it gets my vote."

"You should sit down for a while," he told her. "I don't want those babies to wear you out."

"Those babies," she repeated in a wondering tone. "Oh, Danny, I still can't believe we're having twins."

He dipped his head and kissed her gently. "I can," he said, smiling. "Lady Luck owes me a few. Finding Nick again and marrying you were just the first installment. We've got the rest of our lives to see what else she's got planned."

"Hey, Daddy!" Nick stood on the lawn, hopefully dangling a miniature baseball bat. "Wanna come pitch for me an' Tyler?"

"You bet, buddy," Danny called back. "Give me a minute and I'll be right there." He looked down again at Sydney, nestled in his arms. "The rest of our lives," he repeated as he sought her mouth again. "I love you."

\* \* \* \* \*

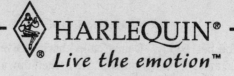